"Rosalind——" Ew............................
as Rosalind checke..........................
saw he wasn't, and l.........................
away. "What——"

"Listen to me, Ewan Gailbraith," she directed as she put her hands on her hips. "I'm willing to hae you pay me court and am flattered as well I should be, but 'tis a wee disgruntled I am, too, and that's a fact."

She shook a finger at his befuddled expression. "Don't look as though you don't ken what I mean. 'Twouldn't hae been overly difficult to give me some forewarning as to your intentions. I do not like to be caught unawares by anything, much less something of such importance." She finished speaking and waited for his reply. He had to understand straight from the start that he shouldn't be making such decisions without at least speaking to her first!

"I like hearing you say my name" was all he said.

"I—Did you not hear what else I said?" Rosalind demanded. " 'Tis vital you understand that I will not hae a husband who makes decisions first and speaks wi' me about them after the fact."

"Aye, Rosalind," he said, rumbling her name as though it were a blessing. "I should hae asked you first so as not to make things awkward for you." He took her hand in his once more, rubbing his thumb along her palm. "I value your thoughts and will seek them often. Does that put your mind at ease?"

No. If anything, my heart is beating fit to burst.

"Aye, that it does." She stepped slightly closer. "And 'tis honored I'll be to hae you come calling on me. . .Ewan."

KELLY EILEEN HAKE has loved reading her whole life, and as she's grown older, she's learned to express her beliefs through the written word. Currently, she is a senior in college, working toward her BA in English. She intends to earn her Single Subject Credential so she can share her love of words with high school students! She likes to cook, take walks, go to college-group activities at her church, and play with her two dogs, Skylar and Tuxedo. God bless!

Books by Kelly Eileen Hake

HEARTSONG PRESENTS
HP640—Taking a Chance
HP664—Chance Adventure
HP672—Chance of a Lifetime
HP721—Through His Grace
HP736—A Time to Plant

Don't miss out on any of our super romances. Write to us at the following address for information on our newest releases and club information.

Heartsong Presents Readers' Service
PO Box 721
Uhrichsville, OH 44683

Or visit www.heartsongpresents.com

A Time to Keep

Kelly Eileen Hake

Heartsong Presents

To God, first and foremost, and to my critique partners and editors, without whom this book would not be what it is today.

A note from the Author:
I love to hear from my readers! You may correspond with me by writing:

Kelly Eileen Hake
Author Relations
PO Box 721
Uhrichsville, OH 44683

ISBN 978-1-59789-658-0

A TIME TO KEEP

All scripture quotations are taken from the King James Version of the Bible.

All of the characters and events in this book are fictitious. Any resemblance to actual persons, living or dead, or to actual events is purely coincidental.

Our mission is to publish and distribute inspirational products offering exceptional value and biblical encouragement to the masses.

PRINTED IN THE U.S.A.

prologue

Ireland 1874

Fifteen-year-old Ewan Gailbraith sidestepped yet another muddy puddle in an Irish thoroughfare. *"Be my braw lad and take good care of your mama for me, son."* His father's words echoed through his mind. *"I'll find good work and send ye the fare to come join me in America."* Ewan stubbornly trudged on in the face of the unseasonable downpour.

"Da left us nigh on a year ago." The lad aimed a fierce kick at a hapless rock as he neared his destination. "Surely this week we'll hae another letter." He drew up short at the old tavern banged together from a motley lot of old boards and prayed that old Ferguson would have an envelope for him.

He swung open the lopsided door. For once his arrival was unannounced by the creaky old hinges, now too waterlogged to protest. Ewan stomped his worn boots on the threshold to dislodge the worst of the mud and then bypassed the hearty welcome of the roaring fire in favor of approaching the tavern owner at the bar.

"Mr. Ferguson," he addressed, drawing up to his full height, "hae you any word from my da this day?" He clenched his teeth as the barkeep looked him over, as much to stop them from chattering as from biting back angry words at the miserable man who drew out his answers as long as the voyage to America.

"Aye." The man reached beneath his scraggly beard, into the pocket of his coat, and drew out a much-handled brown packet. He placed it on the weathered face of the bar and slid it toward the youth.

"Thankee." Ewan manfully resisted the urge to pounce upon the package, instead calmly nudging it off the bar and into the safety of his own threadbare pocket. His hand lingered over the small coin inside before drawing it out, placing it carefully on the bar, and turning away.

"You should warm yoursel' by the fire afore ye step outside again!" the barkeep's wife called to him.

Ewan hesitated, reluctant to waste even a moment before bringing his mam the news from his father, but saw the wisdom of the woman's words. He'd be no good to Mam if he caught a chill and couldn't work. He grudgingly moved toward the warmth of the flames, holding his hands toward the heat. He kept ignoring the curious gazes of the old timers who probably hoped he'd open the envelope before them all and give the town some new gossip to chew over.

He waited until he felt reasonably warmed, if not dry, and headed back into the gray rain. His long stride covered the soggy ground quickly in a bid to stave off the cold on his journey. With each step he took, the packet thumped against his side—a weight that would either ease his burden or add to it. Which would be the case, he knew not. 'Twas not his place to open the envelope before bringing it to his mother. His restless hands clenched at his sides as he neared their small, well-thatched cottage.

"Ewan!" Ma swung open the door and pulled him inside, clucking like a hen as she drew off his jacket and wrapped his hands around a warm mug of water. "I couldn't believe you'd taken off in this weather! What was so important it could not wait a day or two?"

Ewan jerked his chin toward the sopping wet jacket she started to hang on a peg by the door. "It has come, Ma." He watched her blue eyes widen in hope and surprise before her fingers deftly searched his pockets and withdrew the packet.

"Do ye ken what it holds, son?" She turned the envelope over in her hands as though loath to open it.

"Nay. I thought 'twas best we open it together." He put down the mug and walked over to his mother, placing his arm around her shoulders as he towered over her.

At his silent nod, she tore open one side of the envelope and drew two smaller ones from the packet. She opened the thinner of the envelopes first. They stood in silence as they each drank in the strong, sure strokes of his father's hand.

Ewan let loose the breath he hadn't known he'd held. Da was fine and well in America, and he sent his love and hopes that they'd all be together soon. Ewan gave his mother's shoulder a firm squeeze. She then slit open the other envelope to find a significant amount of money. "Oh, Ewan!" Tears of joy ran down his mother's tired face as she looked up at him. "He's well, and we're that much closer to joining him! Why, in another six months or so, we'll have enough to pay both our passages to America."

Ewan looked at his mother's smile and saw the lingering sadness in her eyes. Fine lines had sprung up around her eyes over the last few months and now gave away the disappointment she tried to hide. With each month her husband had been gone, Imogene Gailbraith had lost a bit more of her joy. In another six months, or even an entire year,

Da would not recognize this slight woman as the beloved wife he'd left in his son's care.

Now's the time. 'Tis the right thing to do.

"Ma," Ewan began, taking her chilled hands in his own, "I've given the matter much thought, and I've come to a decision. . ."

one

"Look out!" Brent Freimont practically shoved Rosalind MacLean off the path as he rushed to plunge a bucket into the stream.

Rosalind gasped to see the normally fastidious young man's clothes all askew. "What's wrong?"

"No time." He hurried past her with the now-brimming bucket. Rosalind turned. Whorls of smoke were rising atop the maple trees.

"Fire!" Quickly she filled the unscrubbed pot, still dirty from the morning meal, with water and raced up the path after Brent. Water sloshed over her skirts and bare feet as she went, but she paid no heed. When she reached the line of trees, her suspicions—fueled by the acrid scent of smoke tinged with something even more unpleasant—were confirmed. Someone had set fire to the outhouse.

When she reached the site, several men were already fighting the flames. Dustin Freimont and Isaac and Jakob Albright had obviously rushed over at the first sign of trouble. She handed over the heavy pot with relief. It hadn't been easy hauling it up the hill. She drew in a deep breath and promptly began sputtering. *Not the smartest idea I've ever had,* she admitted to herself when she rushed once again to the stream. Before long, they'd managed to douse the flames.

All that was left was a heap of sodden, smoldering wood—and a lingering stench.

"What on earth happened?" Isaac turned to Brent, outrage written plainly across his handsome features.

"I. . .er. . ." Brent avoided his uncle's gaze only to find Rosalind staring at him in befuddlement. The young man blushed bright red and mumbled something almost incoherent.

"What?" Isaac had plainly missed the whispered confession.

"I was trying to smoke a cigar." Brent spoke more loudly this time, though he seemed no less embarrassed.

"You were *smoking*?!" Dustin Freimont roared, having just come upon the scene in time to hear his son's confession.

"In the *privy*?" Isaac's disbelief more closely mirrored Rosalind's.

"Yes." Brent stared at the wreckage in misery. "I knew better than to try it at home, Pa."

"You would've done well to take that caution a step or two further." Isaac grimaced. "Smoking near anything made of wood is foolish."

Rosalind stepped in. "I think he's learned his lesson." When she caught Brent's adoring gaze, she wished she'd remained silent.

Brent Freimont, a little less than two years her junior, had taken to giving her cow eyes whenever she so much as glanced in his direction. Since she was one of the few single girls in the area who wasn't his younger sister, Rosalind couldn't really blame him for his notice. Then again, she really couldn't encourage him either.

Dustin doled out the punishment. "He'll have learned his lesson once he cleans up this mess and builds a new outhouse."

"What happened?" Rosalind's dad stared at the charred

mess. Mam, followed by Brent's mother, came hard on his heels.

Most days, Rosalind considered the proximity of their homes to be a blessing. When her mother and father had settled this land with the Freimonts and Albrights, they'd agreed to build their homes and barns on the strip of earth joining their properties. She'd grown up with Brent and, later, Marlene. Their parents, Delana and Dustin, lived within spitting distance of her family home. Two generations' worth of each family, all with homes on the same three acres of land.

Not too long ago, it had been three generations on each side. Rosalind looked toward the small cemetery where they'd buried Bernadine, Rawhide, and her Grandda Cade. The only one left was Rosalind's grandmother, Gilda Banning, who'd moved in with the MacLeans when Grandda passed on.

Any way Rose looked on it, she couldn't help but feel all of them were one big family. She knew that her family and Brent's hoped for a match to officially unite them. Try as she might, she couldn't fathom it. Brent seemed as much the scapegrace younger brother to her today as he had when he'd slipped wriggly tadpoles down the back of her dress on his sixth birthday.

Marlene ran up. "Oh, Brent. *Now* what did you do?"

By this point, it seemed as though everyone had gathered at the scene of the crime. Rosalind looked at the familiar faces with fondness, and a part of her wished she could make their dream of a marriage come true. However, that part was drowned out by the loud, insistent voice demanding that she be true to her own heart. Marriage was a lifetime commitment—a commitment she simply couldn't make to the young man who'd just burned down an outhouse.

"Clean it up and build a new one?" Brent's voice jerked

her back to the current problem. "Maybe I should take the opportunity to dig a new one altogether." Anyone who knew Brent could see that the idea of touching the filthy, smelly heap in front of him was enough to make him turn green.

"Good idea." Rosalind's da clapped him on the shoulder. "Clean up this mess and create an entirely new outhouse. Nice to see a man take responsibility for his mistakes and make amends."

Brent rubbed his shoulder sullenly, obviously unwilling to utter another word that might land him more work. One by one, all slipped away to tend to their own chores until Brent was left alone with Rosalind and his sister.

"I'm sorry, Brent." Marlene gave him a commiserating glance even as she looped an arm around Rosalind's shoulders and began to walk away. She bit back a snicker before she added, "This whole thing really stinks!"

She and Rosalind hurried away, failing to hold their giggles. They stopped when they were out of Brent's sight to talk about the contretemps.

"That wasn't very nice, making fun of your brother," Rosalind pointed out.

"There are worse things." Marlene gave a meaningful glance backward before wrinkling her nose. "I just don't understand what goes through his head sometimes."

"Nor do I. Though I wonder"—Rosalind plucked a late-blooming wildflower and twirled it between her fingers—"if others say the same about us."

"Who knows?" Marlene stretched and thought for a moment. "I'd probably say everybody reads us like we're open books."

"Surely not." Rosalind dropped the tiny flower and looked

at the wide blue Montana sky that stretched ahead of them, broken only by the mountain peaks in the distance. "Human beings, like life, are never that simple."

⁂

"This life is simple," Ewan Gailbraith announced to the young man he'd be showing around that day and training for the remainder of the week. "You work hard, keep your mouth shut, an' help others when you can. Don't waste money or flash it around, stay away from Hank's chili, and don't start anything. Only other advice I can give you is to take care o' your tools and they'll take care o' you."

"Yes, sir." The wiry lad twisted his hat in his hands. "I don't mind honest work, so long as it's for honest pay."

"As a wheelwright, you'll be paid well for your skill." Ewan smiled. "In a couple of years, you'll hae enough saved to start a life anywhere you like. That's what most men do."

"Is that what you're planning to do, Mr. Gailbraith?"

Ewan gestured toward a freight car. "That's where we keep the raw materials." *When and where will I leave the railroad and begin my own life?* He kept talking business in an effort to distract himself from the question he refused to answer. "We build makeshift forges when and where we need them as the railroad builds from town to town. For the first week, you'll be transporting finished items and presized strips down to where the track is being laid. It won't be too much longer before we hae to set up the forge farther down."

"I thought there was a small town a little ways farther down."

"There is. Saddleback is where we'll set up our next base. We'll be continuing the main line an' beginning an offshoot running through there, so you can count on staying there a while. You'll end up trying your hand as farrier before long, I'd warrant."

"I apprenticed with a farrier for the last year." The young man sounded a bit more confident now.

"All to the good. I do both jobs myself." Ewan stopped for a moment and spoke more carefully. "Now, if you were apprenticing, why didn't you see it through?"

"My master drank too much one night and fell in the horse trough. I found him the next morning."

"Overfond o' t' bottle, eh?" Ewan gave the youth a measuring look. "There are some here who share that weakness. You seem a bright lad, but I'll offer you this warning: Don't indulge in drink, gaming, or some o' the loose women who follow the railroad. Any one of those vices will take your money and leave you feeling ill. I don't tolerate that sort of behavior from my men. Understood?"

"Yes, sir." The fellow stood a little taller. "I never held much stock by those ways myself."

"I'm glad to hear it." Ewan turned and continued walking. "Honest values and hard work will take you farther than the railroad itself ever can."

two

"The railroad will take this town and build it into a city." Rosalind could practically have danced upon the words she spoke to her father. He didn't respond while he ate the mid-morning snack she'd brought to his smithy. "Think of it—the workers who lay the rails are not so far off. I heard that they'll have reached us before the week is out."

"I'm thinkin' on it more an' more wi' each passing day, Rosey-mine." Da wore an expression she'd seen before only when he looked at his son. Pride tinged with regret for what could have been.

She and Luke were the joys of her father's life, but Da had hoped to pass on his trade to his son. With Luke's weak lungs, he would never stand at his father's forge, carrying on an age-old family tradition. Yes, she knew well the wistful gleam that crept into Da's eyes as he spoke of the progress of the "iron horse." But what could he possibly regret when they'd be linked at long last to the world beyond Saddleback? What opportunities lay at the other end of those rails?

"Da? What is it, exactly, you've been thinking on?"

"Sit down wi' me for a moment, lass." He gestured to a bench in the corner and sat down heavily. " 'Tis time and past for us to speak on a few matters."

"Da?" Worry sparked in her heart at the lines on her father's brow.

"Don't fret so, Rosey-mine. 'Tis nothing so dire as you may

imagine." Her father drew a deep breath. "It seems to me as though 'twas only yesterday your ma came out here to join me. Her showing up wi' you in her arms was the sweetest moment of my life. I remember it so clearly. But I look on the memories which filled the passing years, and I know better. I see the stamp of time on your lovely face, Rosey, and can't deny that you've become a woman grown. If I were honest, I would say that I've known it for quite some time now."

Dread thudded in Rosalind's heart. Surely Da wouldn't tell her she must choose a husband and move on? Aye, most lasses wed long before their nineteenth year, but couldn't he see that it wasn't the right time for her?

"You are a beauty, just like your mother." Da's sudden smile brought a welcome rush of relief. "But with that beauty comes danger. A lovely lass without the protection of a husband can be a target for evil men."

"Da!" Rosalind burst out, desperate to stop his flow of words. "I know everyone expects me to make my choice soon, but I can't! Not when all I've ever known is this small piece of the world and the familiar faces on it! The railroad will give me the opportunity to see a bit more, meet new people, afore I settle down. Would you deny me that chance?"

"Nay, Rosey-mine, I wouldn't. Your ma and Delana cherish hopes that you'll choose to wed Brent. Nay, don't speak now." He held up one massive hand as though to ward off her alarm. " 'Tis your choice to make, daughter, but to my way of thinking, Brent 'tisn't the man for you. If he were, you would hae settled on him long ago."

Rosalind nodded, half ashamed at the admission she'd be letting down her mother but half relieved that her father understood and accepted her decision.

"I'll hae no part in shoving my lassie out of our home and into the arms of a man she doesn't love as deeply as I cherish your ma. And, were I to be completely honest, I don't know what we'd do wi'out you." Her father's grin made Rosalind's own smile falter.

Here, then, was the heart of the matter. Da knew she longed to explore the opportunities the railroad would bring, but he was reminding her of her responsibilities here at home. She helped Ma with the garden, cooking, housework, and sewing when she wasn't taking meals to Da or watching over Luke. If she followed her own dreams, she'd be leaving her family behind—and they needed her. Rosalind struggled against the sense of confinement pressing in upon her. She'd never abandon them, no matter what it cost her. She opened her mouth to assure her father that he could rely on her.

"What I mean to say is that we love you dearly, Rosey-mine, and I mean to warn you about the changes the railroad will bring." Her father's serious expression bore into her.

"Oh, I already know much of what to expect." Her enthusiasm rushed to the tip of her tongue. " 'Twill bring many people—farmers, traders, railroad officials, and more—to our small town. The number of families will swell, and our ability to send goods and receive modern niceties will increase dramatically. Should we want to visit Fort Benton or Virginia City, 'twill take naught but a fraction of the time we'd spend on horseback to arrive there and journey back. New friends, adventures just a ride away, and shorter waits for everything! The railroad is a marvel, Da. 'Twill change everything." *And I can hardly wait!*

" 'Tis glad I am to hear you've been thinking on the matter so seriously." Da nodded his approval. "Is that all you have to say on it, or will you be able to tell me of some o' the drawbacks the railroad brings along with all that shining opportunity?"

"Drawbacks?" Rosalind felt her brow crease as she considered this. "I suppose 'twill be awkward meeting new people and drawing them into our small community, but we'll all be the better for it, Da. And along wi' the opportunity will come more work for you—the more people, the more demand for your smithy, I know. I wouldna like to see you o'erworked." She gave him a stern glance.

"Nor would I," he agreed, a grin teasing the corners of his lips. "Though the work and pay will bring benefits as well—medicine for Luke, some of those newfangled laundry contraptions for your mam, delicious treats for us to sample at the general store. . ." He paused until he caught his daughter's eye. "And fine, fancy young men to turn a pretty lass's head."

"Oh, Da." Rosalind tried to ignore the heat rising to her cheeks.

"Now, you wouldna be trying to tell your old da the thought hadna crossed your mind?" His teasing made the blush deepen.

"I—" Rosalind's response was mercifully cut short by an interruption.

A tall, burly man stood in the entryway, powerful shoulders blocking out much of the day's light. Even though Rosalind couldn't see his shadowed features, she knew this wasn't one of her neighbors. It seemed as though the railroad—and the changes to come—had arrived.

❧

Ewan blinked, trying to adjust his vision to the dimness inside the smithy. Slowly, he began to take note of the way things were set up. He liked what he saw.

The stone forge stood about forty inches high and forty inches square—large enough for big work and deep enough for the fire to most efficiently use the air from the great leather and wood bellows. He'd seen from the outside of the structure that the forge's chimney boasted a brick hood to carry out smoke and fine ash.

The anvil and slag tub stood close enough at hand to be immediately useful, but with a good, clear working space around them. The front and sides of the forge held racks and rings to hold hammers, tongs, chisels, files, and other tools. This in and of itself was not unusual; the fact that the tools had been put in their proper place immediately after use was. Most blacksmiths heaped their tools on the lip of the forge, having to quickly dig out the needed implement from beneath several of its fellows before continuing work.

Altogether, it was a well-built, well-stocked, and well-kept smithy far above and beyond what he'd expected to find in the depths of the Montana wilderness. Ewan tamped down an unexpected spurt of longing. It had been a long time since he'd worked in an honest smithy instead lugging a cast-iron patent forge from work site to work site. The only advantage of a patent forge, in Ewan's opinion, was the mobility so highly prized by the railroad.

"Will you be needing anything now?" The resident blacksmith, a tall man who spoke with the lilt of home, stepped in front of Ewan.

Ewan shook himself free of the unbidden memories before speaking. "Perhaps." He looked around frankly, nodding in admiration, before continuing. "I'm Ewan Gailbraith, and I work wi' Montana Central as their head blacksmith. I step in to help wi' a bit o' the work of farrier and wheelwright."

Ewan allowed his syllables to boast of his own Irish heritage. "We had some men decide to stay back at Benton, and I find myself a bit shorthanded as we make our way toward your town."

At the approval Ewan demonstrated for the smithy's workshop, the man seemed to thaw a bit.

"Now, then, that's a shame." The smith's eyes held a spark of interest. He gave an assessing look in return for Ewan's own appraisal.

"We're miles away from here, and the company will be moving t' make camp in this area any day now." Ewan noted the flicker of unease that crossed the older man's features as he quickly glanced over his shoulder to the corner of the shop.

It didn't take much to see what concerned the man. A lovely lass stood in the corner, her demure pose belied by the avid interest on her face as she listened to their conversation. Within the darkness of the smithy, the colors of her braided hair and lively eyes were shadowed, but there was no hiding her lithesome shape and obvious intelligence. Ewan caught himself before his glance could become rude and resolutely returned his focus to the blacksmith.

" 'Tis good to know when we can expect the chaos ahead." The blacksmith thrust his hand toward Ewan. "Arthur MacLean, blacksmith of Saddleback."

"I'd a suspicion." Ewan grinned and returned the man's firm grip as he pumped his hand in welcome.

"This is my daughter, Rosalind." Arthur gestured toward the lass, and she stepped forward with lively grace.

" 'Tis grand to meet you, Mr. Gailbraith."

Ewan noted a pair of bright blue eyes framed by a riot of fiery curls. "And you, Miss MacLean." Intensely aware of

her father's scrutiny, Ewan greeted her with all the formality a wary papa could require, even as he tried to hide his astonishment. Why had no one seen fit to warn him or the other supervisors that this small, out-of-the-way settlement held at least one pretty, unmarried female? This would greatly complicate things, as the workers saw precious few women along the work trail.

"Now that you've been introduced to Mr. Gailbraith, run home and tell your mam to be expecting a guest for dinner." Arthur MacLean folded his arms across his massive chest. "For now, he and I have some business to discuss."

Ewan refused to give in to the urge to watch Rosalind MacLean leave the smithy. He waited in silence until he could be sure the girl was out of earshot.

"Mr. MacLean," Ewan spoke before her father had the chance, "before we discuss smithy business, I would like to have a word about your daughter." He waited for the man's leery nod. Obviously, Arthur MacLean was a man who liked to have all the facts before he made a judgment. That boded well.

Ewan searched for words to put the matter delicately. Finding none, he plunged forward. "In large cities, men who so choose may find. . .companionship. However, it has been long days since we were at such a place. Lonely, less-than-civilized men will be descending upon your town by the dozens, and I will plainly tell you that I have fears concerning the well-being of your daughter."

"As do I." The man uncrossed his arms and rubbed the back of his neck. "We've another young lass or two in the area, as well. The only men they've ever known, they've grown up with. This is a small town filled wi' friends and extended family. None of the girls has any notion of how to handle strange men."

"I'm certain that you are able to protect your own, sir, but I hope that I may trust you t' warn the others of your community t' be diligent about watching o'er the misses." Ewan gave the man a meaningful glance. "I'll give the men a stern talking-to and set up what measures I can."

"I'll be taking your word on that, Mr. Gailbraith."

"Please, call me Ewan."

"Ewan. And you're to call me Arthur." MacLean gave a decisive nod. "Now that we've reached an agreement concerning what I deem the most important matter we could discuss, let's get down to business."

&

"Mam!" Rosalind rushed into the house. "Da sent me to tell you we'll be having a guest for dinner!"

"A guest?" Luke piped the question first.

"Aye. A Mr. Gailbraith, smith for the railroad. He came to Da's shop just now. He was still there when I left." Rosalind rushed about, tidying the flowers in a cracked mug, polishing a spot on the ornate metalwork of the stove grate, whisking dishes onto the table. "I'll pop in a batch of biscuits from the dough I made this morning. They should be finished in time."

"Such a flurry," Mam marveled as she stirred the stew. "Is there aught you should be telling your mam before this important visitor walks through our door?"

"He's come to offer Da work, I think." Rosalind slid the biscuits into the bread oven. "And he brings news that the railroad men will be here any day!"

"I see."

Rosalind stilled as Grandmam caught her by the wrist and addressed her brother. "Luke, would you please go to the springhouse and fetch some butter and milk?" Once he was out of sight, she turned her sharp gaze upon her granddaughter.

Mam was the one who spoke up. "Rose, there's something we'd been meaning to speak wi' you about. 'Tis a delicate matter, but the time has come upon us sooner than expected." Mam had the same long look Da had worn scant minutes ago.

"Yes, Mam?" Rosalind wondered if it had to do with the same topic. *I hope it doesn't. Lord, I'm not ready to tell her my decision against Brent.*

"From all your talk, I know you are thinking that the railroad will bring many wondrous things—and so it shall. Yet the men who will build the rail line may not be so very wondrous, daughter." Mam paused meaningfully. "You've been sheltered here, surrounded only by friends and family. Now, strangers will begin to arrive in our midst—men who may not be as honorable or God-fearing as those you know. You must hae a care, Rose, not to become enamored wi' them or fall prey to any unscrupulous tricks. Be wary of these strangers, and guard your heart and mind, as well as your physical self. Do you understand me, Rose?"

"Aye, Mam." Rose nodded faintly. "Such dark thoughts about our fellow men, though! It puts a caution into my heart to hear you, who I've never heard say a harsh word over any soul, warn me so."

"See that you take heed. From now on, you are not to walk anywhere on your lonesome. You will hae your father, brother, myself, or someone known and trusted by us in your company at all times."

"Mam!" Rosalind couldn't stop the dismayed cry. *I already*

take Luke wi' me almost everywhere I go, and I'm always at the house or the smithy. The only moments I hae for my own thoughts and dreams seem to be while I'm traveling from one place to another. I didn't think they could clip my wings any further! Oh, heavenly Father, I don't see how I'm to bear it!

"I know 'tis a sacrifice on your part, made necessary through no fault of your own, dear." Mam rubbed her hand down Rosalind's back. "Lovely young women usually learn to take such precautions at a far earlier age. You've had more freedom here than most."

Freedom? I've lived in the same small area my entire life! Until now my whole world consisted solely of Saddleback. Now, at my first opportunity to see anything different, I'm pulled ever closer to the bosom of my family. She paused, trying to see it from their view. *Da warned me. Mam and Grandmam did the same. . . .*

Lord, is this Your way? Parents protect their children, and though I feel I'm no longer a child, I know that they ask these things for what they deem my own good. Your Word tells me to honor my father and mother, and so I shall.

"I'll not go anywhere unescorted, Mam." The very words seemed to constrict her, but Rosalind knew that to struggle against her parents' wishes would only make them tie her still more tightly.

"I'm glad to see you being so sensible, Rose. 'Tis a sign of your maturity. Someday, not too far off, you'll hae a home of your own, and our little chats will be about how to rear your little ones." Mam, stirring the pot once again, had her back turned to Rosalind and so could not notice her daughter's expression of worry. She kept speaking. "If this man is a smith, he'll have a hearty appetite. Best see if you can slip in one more batch of biscuits, dear."

Rosalind smoothed back the irrepressible wisps of curls around her face before pulling the fragrant golden biscuits from the oven.

"Smells wonderful." Da's voice preceded him and Mr. Gailbraith, giving them last-minute warning.

"It does indeed," Mr. Gailbraith agreed, taking off his hat as he entered.

"Ewan Gailbraith, this is Kaitlin, my bonny bride." Da put a loving arm around his wife's waist. "And her mam, Gilda Banning. This is my son, Luke, and you've already met my daughter."

" 'Tis pleased I am to make your acquaintance, Mrs. MacLean, Mrs. Banning." He gave a slight bow to Mam and Grandmam. Then, turning in Rosalind's direction, he nodded his head and said, "Good to see you again, Miss MacLean." With a smile, he greeted Luke, pumping his hand heartily.

Rosalind busied herself, refusing to show any undue interest in the man now sitting at their table. The light of day revealed his hair to be deepest ebony, and his smiling eyes glinted a good Irish green. A strong jaw squared his face and framed a ready smile. All in all, he was even more handsome than she'd supposed. This, then, was the first stranger in their midst.

He doesn't seem dangerous at all. There is something in him, aside from his broad shoulders and arms made thick from hard work, to remind me of Da. Perhaps this is the reason Mam warned me—I do not make a practice of seeing darkness in another. I know nothing of this man yet would be liable to trust him already. His very ease of manner and handsome appearance must make him every bit as dangerous as Mam fears these men may be. Now that I've been warned, I'll be sure to watch myself around him. For all I know, he's a threat.

three

Miss Rosalind MacLean, Ewan decided, was a serious threat to his peace of mind. Standing near the window with the sunshine pouring a golden blessing upon her fiery locks and creamy skin, she delighted his eye and dismayed his heart. What red-blooded man among his workers would be able to resist such a siren? The light blue skirts of her dress swayed gently as she brought a basket of perfectly baked biscuits to the table.

No, no, no. Please, Lord, tell me she didn't bake those biscuits. Show me that she burns any morsel of food she tries to prepare. When she speaks, let her be missing a few teeth. At the very least, let her be clumsy enough to knock things over! When she gracefully set the hot biscuits down and gave him a soft smile full of perfect teeth, Ewan despaired. It took him a few moments to regroup with a few more cheery thoughts.

Perhaps she laughs like a donkey, eats with poor manners, or displays signs of becoming a nag. Maybe she isn't usually so clean as today or is content t' shirk her chores. She could have harsh words for others or be one o' those babbling women who causes men to shudder. There are still numerous off-putting faults she may possess to discourage suitors.

One-half hour, one blessing, two bowls of stew, and three lighter-than-air biscuits later, Ewan leaned back. He watched as Rosalind MacLean graciously cleared the table, leaving a bewitching scent of roses and the silvery chime of her laughter as she passed. She'd been respectful to her parents, kind to her brother, welcoming yet reserved toward him, and maintained neither silence nor continuous chatter. Ewan stifled a groan, masking his discomfort by patting his almost-too-full stomach.

" 'Twas a delicious dinner, and I'm much obliged t' you all. I haven't eaten a meal so grand in ages."

"Will you be leaving, then, so soon?" Arthur sounded genuinely disappointed.

"I've work to attend to, and I'd not want to be holdin' anyone else from theirs." Ewan eyed what seemed a veritable mountain of dirty dishes.

"You can't make the time for some coffee and a bit o' shortbread, Mr. Gailbraith?" Rosalind's clear, cool voice washed over him.

"I *am* powerful fond of shortbread," he admitted. "And I wanted to ask about something before I left."

"Yes?" Arthur's undivided attention seemed overly intent. "What can we tell you?"

"When and where is Sunday meeting held hereabouts?"

"It moves around," Luke MacLean said.

"Oh?" Ewan smiled at the lad. Had Arthur not already mentioned his son was twelve, Ewan would have estimated the slight lad to have reached only eight or nine years. Perhaps his small stature explained his absence from the smithy. He'd need to gain more height and breadth to do a blacksmith's work. "And where would a man be finding it come this Lord's day?"

"That'd be at the Freimonts' place, just north of us." Kaitlin passed him a mug of strong, hot coffee as Rosalind placed a plate of shortbread on the table.

"We meet at nine o'clock sharp," she advised. "Now, the Albrights hae the largest house hereabouts, but all the same we'll be on benches under God's own Montana sky. If you're late, you won't manage a seat."

" 'Tis glad I am to hear that you're a God-fearing man, Gailbraith." Arthur gave him a hearty clap on the shoulder. "If the railroad brings more like you, I'm thinking we'll hae no need t' regret its arrival."

"I can't speak for the others." Ewan felt the need to be honest. "They're rough men. They all work hard, eat as much as they can, as fast as they can, and seek diversion where they may. Some have been following the railroad for so long they can't be held to the same standard as city folk."

"All men should be held to the standard of God," Rosalind spoke up. "So long as they're honest and treat others as they'd like to be treated, we'll get along fine."

Ewan's heart sank. *How can she be so naïve? I just warned her that they're hard men who lack manners and don't care for niceties. There is no way to be plainer wi'out being too blunt for delicate female ears. Lord, please see to it that her parents discuss the matter wi' her!*

"Unfortunately," he began cautiously, "the law of the railroad camp seems t' be more along the lines o' every man for himself. The men hold certain loyalties to their work crews and such, but in the long run, they'll take what they want as long as they think they can get away wi' it."

"We'll all be sure to keep that in mind." Kaitlin sent her daughter a meaningful look, and Ewan rested more easily.

"How came you to be out in the Montana Territory?" He reached for a piece of buttery shortbread that melted almost as soon as he tasted it.

"Ah, now there's a story for those romance novels my daughter has a way of sneaking." Arthur's words made Rosalind blush as pink as the flower for which she was named, but it seemed only Ewan had noticed. "I trekked out here nigh on two decades ago wi' naught but a pair of friends and a heavy load of determination."

"Aye. Naught else on account of him leaving his bride behind wi' her folks." Kaitlin's glance held more love than reproof, but the revelation that Rosalind's father had left his wife to travel across America struck a horribly familiar chord. The shortbread turned to sawdust as he tried to force it down his throat, and he slugged some coffee to wash it down. The bitter memories were harder to swallow. As long as he lived, Ewan would never understand how the promise of a new land could call a man away from his loved ones, leaving them alone and unprotected. *That's not fair,* he amended. *Arthur left his wife with her parents, so she wasna alone.*

"Imagine my surprise when I discovered I was wi' child." Kaitlin beamed and hugged her daughter close. "Our own wee lassie came into this world loud and strong. She would hae made you proud, Arthur."

"She already has, Katy-me-love. My only regret 'tis that I could not share the moment." Arthur's smile dimmed. "'Tis a petty sorrow in the face of so many blessings, but one I will take to my grave regardless."

"Now, Da"—Rosalind left her mother's side to kiss her father's cheek—"you may not hae been there for my first months of life, but your provision and love hae seen me through the years."

"Ah, I love you, Rosey-mine, just as I loved you when I caught my first glimpse of you being held in the arms of your

mam, fresh from traveling thousands of miles to my side."
He patted his daughter's delicate hand. "The Lord safely
delivered two blessings that day."

"How wonderful for you," Ewan choked out, his own loss
harsher in the face of their shared love. "So many never make
it t' the promised land or to the waiting arms o' their loved
ones."

"Too true." Rosalind's eyes held a compassion that seemed
to sear his soul. "What of you, Mr. Gailbraith? Where is your
family while you follow the railroad to provide for them?"

"I cannot say where my da is, the Lord took my mam o'er a
decade ago, and I hae no wife." Ewan, aware of how gruff his
voice sounded, summoned a semblance of a grin. " 'Tis good
to see that you value what you're so blessed to have."

He shoved away from the table and strode to the door,
plunking his hat on his head. "Thank you for your welcome
and hospitality, Mrs. MacLean. I've much work to finish this
day, so I must be going. I look forward to working wi' you,
Arthur. Luke, Miss MacLean." With a tip of his hat, he walked
out without a backward glance.

≈

"Mr. Gailbraith seems nice enough," Rosalind ventured as she
and her mother cleared the dinner table. Luke had volunteered
to go to the Albrights' place and see about arranging an apple
bee. The tree branches drooped, heavy with the weight of ripe
fruit, but Rosalind felt the weight of unanswered questions.

"Aye." Mam's short agreement made Rosalind relax for
but a moment. "*Seems* is just the right word to be using to
describe him."

"His manners 'tweren't off-putting, he showed Da proper
respect, and he asked after Sunday meeting." Rosalind stopped

wiping down the board. "What concerns you?"

"What type of man does not know where his own kith and kin lay their heads?" Mam stoked the fire with more vigor than was strictly necessary. "A good son looks to his father in his twilight years, and that's a fact."

"We cannot know his reasons, Mam. There could be a perfectly good explanation." *Why am I defending the man? I've barely met him, and yet he's the first new man in town. Will Mam be so suspicious of everyone, or is it Mr. Gailbraith in particular?*

"Will you be telling me that a man with an honest explanation would all but bolt from the table?" Mam shook her head. "There's something amiss there."

"Mayhap." Rosalind went silent as she gathered the trenchers and pot to scrub by the brook.

"Be sure to fetch Luke afore you make your way to the stream."

"Yes, Mam." She stopped at the threshold when she thought of another question. "Is there aught else you find to dislike about him, or are we to be wary simply because he's not our neighbor?"

"I've already spoken wi' you, Rose. A young miss cannot be too careful around men, especially strange ones." Mam shooed her out the door, but Rosalind caught the statement made under her breath. "Particularly ones as handsome as Mr. Gailbraith."

Ah, so I'm not the only one to notice his fine looks, Rosalind mused. *And I suppose Mam saw the dark storm in the deep green of his gaze when he spoke on his family. No mother, no wife, no father in his life. 'Twouldn't surprise me a bit if 'twas pure loneliness as made him pull away, after hearing all about our happy family. It takes strength of a different sort than a blacksmith usually needs to live such a solitary life.*

"Rose!" Luke's voice made her look around sharply. Her little brother loped down the path toward her, cutting her search short.

"Hello, Luke. I've come to seek your escort to the stream."

Her brother caught on to her joke and replied with an exaggerated bow. "Of course I will escort you, miss." He took the heavy pot from her hands and walked beside her, the top of his head barely reaching her elbow. At twelve years, he should have come close to his petite sister's shoulder.

Rosalind shoved the worry aside and listened to her brother's uneven breathing, noting a hint of a wheeze creeping into the sound as they passed the hayfields. "How are you?" She tried to keep her tone light.

"Now then, you wouldna be fussing o'er me, would you?" He teased a smile on to her face. "Surely not, on account of how you know of my hay fever. 'Twill ease when we near the brook."

And so it did. The harsh, raspy sound Rosalind so dreaded had faded away by the time they knelt by the cool, clear water. She watched as her brother scooped up some damp sand and scrubbed enthusiastically.

To those who didn't know of the difficulties Luke suffered from hay fever, running, smoke, and cold weather, it would be all too easy to see a healthy young boy. In truth, Luke's weak lungs made it so he could never take up blacksmithing, run with other children, help with the haying, or play overlong in the snow. At those times, his fight to breathe was nothing short of terrifying for those who loved him. And love him she did. Rose would do anything to see her brother happy and healthy.

"Hey!" Luke glowered at her in indignation, his scowl made comical by drops of the water she'd just splashed him with. At her grin, his anger disappeared, replaced by a crafty gleam. "Rose, if you mean to splash someone, you really should try to do a better job."

"Oh, now?" Rosalind shot to her feet, thinking to back away before her brother could retaliate. Too late. She blinked and sputtered after he doused her with an impressive splash. She planted her hands on her hips and glared at her brother. "And who's to say I meant to splash you, Lucas Mathias MacLean?"

"Ah." Luke didn't look at all repentant as he gave his thoughtful reply. "Then I suppose it serves you right for your carelessness."

Rosalind, unable to think of a suitable rejoinder, gave in to her brother's logic. "Why, you may have a point."

"Most usually I do."

"In that case, may I suggest you work on the virtue of humility"—Rosalind gathered the wooden trenchers—"so that others don't think poorly of you when you use your intelligence."

"Yes, Rose." His downcast eyes and soft voice made him the very picture of a humble young man—until he peeked up at his sister. "How was that?"

She couldn't help but laugh. He joined in. Still laughing together, they started for home. Rosalind's merriment dried up when they passed the freshly cut hayfields and Luke's breathing grew raspy once more.

four

"This is the patent forge supplied by the Montana Central Railroad Company." Ewan gestured toward the heavy equipment. "Thank you again for letting us set up near your forge. 'Tis a good location for the work we'll be doing in the area, and 'twill simplify things whilst we work together."

"Aye, 'tis no trouble." Arthur circled the "portable" forge, a monstrosity of cast iron. "Grand, the way you don't have to build a new forge every time you pick up and move. Comparatively, this sets up right quick."

"True enough," Ewan agreed. "But no one will convince me that a good stone or brick-built forge 'tisn't the very best to work wi'."

"I'll not even be tryin'." Arthur straightened up. "All the same, 'tis an incredible piece of modern machinery."

"Sure as shootin'." The young man named Johnny cast a fond eye on the forge. "She's a beaut, that's what I say."

"There's work enough to go around." Ewan looked to the makeshift hitching posts where dozens of horses were tied, waiting to be inspected for shoeing.

"Let's get to it." Arthur walked confidently over to chestnut mare, running his hand over her withers and crooning for a moment before inspecting her hooves, one by one.

While Johnny worked to make the fire hot enough to temper iron, Ewan began with a tall bay. *Not a day too soon.* The gelding's hooves had overgrown the shoe by a long shot

34

and would certainly begin to crack painfully if let go any longer.

He removed the too-smooth shoes one by one, cleaning each hoof before trimming it down. He fetched one of the shoes Johnny had heating over the fire and set it on the hard wall of the hoof, cautiously using hammer and tongs to shape the pliable metal to the best fit possible before nailing it in place.

Ewan worked efficiently, his job made simpler by Johnny's aid. All the same, he remained careful to soothe each horse and keep a wary eye on the back legs as he worked. Many a blacksmith, overconfident in his expertise, had become careless. Such men received a harsh kick to the ribs or skull and were often fortunate to survive at all. Ewan noted approvingly that Arthur showed the same awareness and appropriate caution. Things were going well.

"What say you to a bite of dinner?" Arthur spoke up only after Ewan had finished shoeing a strawberry roan. "My wife and daughter packed enough for all of us."

"Aah!" Johnny straightened out. "I was beginning to fear you'd hear the rumble of my stomach between the blows of the hammer."

They settled in the shade of a large tree whose leaves, in bright shades of orange and deep red, covered the ground more than the branches. Arthur passed around cold bacon sandwiches and apples.

"How long have you worked wi' the railroad, then?" Arthur took a mammoth bite, almost halving his first sandwich.

"Just started a few days back." Johnny swallowed audibly before he reached for his canteen. "Ewan's been training me."

"Is that so?" Arthur eyed Ewan speculatively. "And how

long has it been since you enjoyed the comforts of home?"

"Too long." Ewan shifted against the tree trunk, finding a less lumpy resting place for his shoulder. "Years, in fact."

"Years, eh?" Arthur savored a sip of cool water before popping the rest of his sandwich in his mouth and reaching for another. "Were you ever wi' the Northern Pacific Railroad Company?"

"Aye." Ewan frowned as he polished off his first sandwich. "I moved on after I realized the company didn't share my priorities."

"The Last Spike Snub?" Johnny stopped eating to stare at Ewan. "Is that whole mess what made you decide to leave?"

" 'Twas a symptom of the overall problem, aye." Ewan sampled his apple. The crisp fruit gave a tart but sweet flavor. *Tart and sweet, the same combination offered by old memories.*

"I heard tell of that about three years ago, but I don't know the details." Arthur poured some water into his cupped palm and combed it through his hair. "I'd like to hear your version of it."

" 'Twas a raging fiasco, to tell the truth." Ewan closed his eyes, remembering the upswell of righteous anger against the company. "I know that the men had been pushed to finish the tracks before the worst of winter hit. When the two lines were ready to be joined, the owners of the company arranged a grand occasion to announce their success in bringing the railroad as far as the Montana Territory."

"That much I know," Johnny affirmed. "What I don't understand is how a happy event upset so many people."

" 'Twasn't the meeting of the railroads that caused problems," Ewan clarified. " 'Twas the way the company treated its own guests.

"Several important people, wealthy, powerful, renown, were invited to meet at the Helena depot. These particular guests were transported to the site in the finest railroad cars o' the Northern Pacific. Sumptuous dining cars, Pullman sleeping compartments, and more were provided for these favored few.

"The bulk of the guests, however, weren't so fortunate. Dignitaries, people prominent in only the Montana Territory, and large landowners were also invited but left t' find their own transportation. They waited in the cold for the delayed train full of the other guests to arrive. At long last, the ceremony began."

"So they were upset that they weren't given the same treatment." Arthur mulled over his thoughts. "Since they were already in the Montana area, it stands to reason they would need to arrange their own transport."

"Sounds to me like some uppity folks got their noses out of joint over nuthin', if you ask me." Johnny rolled his eyes. "Can't imagine such a fuss over something so minor."

"That wasn't the end of it," Ewan warned before continuing. "Once the event actually began, only those who had traveled on the train cars were allowed inside the pavilion area t' hear the speakers. Everyone else was made to crowd in behind the platform, straining to hear. Even worse, the majority o' the seats inside were empty."

Ewan noted Arthur's darkening frown and nodded. "After the speeches were made and the spike driven in, 'twas time to dine. Everyone expected a grand feast after traveling miles to celebrate the occasion and waiting for hours in the cold. Many had day-long trips home t' look forward to."

"Stands to reason," Arthur proclaimed. "After being treated so poorly, they deserved some reward for their trouble, particularly as invited guests."

"And so they expected." Ewan paused to let that sink in. "The final blow was that only the train passengers, warmly ensconced in the new dining cars, were allowed t' take part in the feast. The multitude of guests—those who had traveled so far to bear witness to this historic occasion, waited patiently through delays, and suffered a grievous slight throughout the ceremonies—were told to go home. Precious few of those guests had even thought t' bring food, and a great many went hungry that day."

"Shameful." Johnny's jaw clenched. "I knew that a lot of people felt like it was a waste of time and that they'd been insulted, but I never knew the exact particulars. I don't read all that much, truth be told."

"Out here the news comes slowly. When we heard about it, there were far fewer details." Arthur turned his level gaze to Ewan. "You were right to sever ties wi' such people. It speaks to the strength of your character."

" 'Twasn't as though I were the only one who left." Ewan shrugged. "And I'm of the opinion that Montana Central hired me more for the strength of my arm." With that, he got to his feet. "Let's get back to work."

❧

"It'll never work." Rosalind flopped down in the barn's fresh, fragrant hayloft. Isaac had walked Marlene over. The two girls had finagled permission to snatch some leisure time, since they saw each other far less often now.

"Sure it will!" Marlene settled in next to her. "It feels as though we've hardly even seen each other in the past fortnight! Both our families have watched us with eagle eyes since the railroad men started lurking around."

"Wi' good reason. Some seem like good men, but others give me an uneasy feeling," Rosalind admitted. "Besides, it won't last forever. The railroad will hae to keep steaming along eventually."

"Do you really want it to take all the eligible young men away with it?" Marlene sat up straight. "Our very first opportunity to make new friends and meet men who aren't our neighbors, and it's all but snatched from us!"

"I'm not going to do it." Rosalind sifted a few smaller pieces of hay between her fingers. "I won't say I'm going to meet wi' you while you say you'll meet wi' me and we both hie off to find adventure. No matter how you try to justify it, 'tis dishonest and unsafe."

"You're right. Besides," Marlene huffed as she settled back into the hay, "we'd be found out before long, even if I could actually tell an untruth like it was nothing."

"If nothing worse happened," Rosalind reminded her best friend, glad to see her letting go of the rash idea. Usually they saw eye to eye despite their three-year age difference, but occasionally, Marlene's youthful exuberance got the better of her. "Although, I've had a few thoughts of my own. . . ."

"Do tell!"

"There is one way I can think of that will allow us to be useful, see each other regularly, and spend a bit of time with the railroad men in a protected setting." Rosalind paused until her friend nudged her arm.

"Out with it, Rose. You can't keep me waiting up here forever, and we need to work out the entire plan!"

"Our fathers wouldn't argue if we took in laundry and mending to earn some money. We're of the age where we'll be setting up our own homes soon." Rosalind shared a conspiratorial glance with Marlene. "Or if that idea doesn't tickle your fancy, I should think we could talk a few of our family men into making some rough picnic tables for us to run an outdoor café. We could use the summer oven and an open fire to make home-cooked meals for all those bachelors."

"That," Marlene sighed, "is surely the most brilliant thing I've ever heard you say, Rosalind MacLean. "No one could possibly object to such a worthwhile—and profitable—endeavor!"

"And I prefer almost any chore over laundry," Rosalind added.

"Me, too. I love the feel of clean clothes and sheets, but it's such monotonous, long, hot work, no matter what the season. Soap making is almost as bad." Marlene grimaced, then seemed to realize she'd gotten away from the important topic. "We'll have to convince our parents that we'll finish our own chores. How do we manage that?"

"We'll still milk the cows, gather the eggs, and help wi' breakfast in the morning. If we suggest that everyone eat the dinner we make, our mothers won't have to make any." Rosalind spoke the thoughts aloud as they came into her head. "We'll still help wi' supper and do our sewing in the evenings at the hearth. I suppose that leaves doing the weekly laundry on Saturday as the big problem. We could close down that day and the Lord's day—and only run the outdoor diner five days a week."

"Five days a week sounds good to me." Marlene gave a sly smile. "The men we're interested in will come to Sunday meeting anyway."

"Exactly." Rosalind let Marlene think she was simply bored

and boy-crazy. *No one needs to know that I'll be saving the money I earn so I can travel on that railroad someday.*

"Let's go talk to Aunt Kaitlin now!" Marlene scrambled down the ladder in record time, looking up at Rosalind expectantly.

"You can't seem overly excited," Rosalind cautioned as she descended the ladder. "If you're too eager, they'll think it a whim and shut us down before we even open. We have to present it in just the right way—thoughtfully and reasonably. Show them we're aware of the responsibility we'll be taking on and we're ready for it."

"When did you get so wise, Rose?" Marlene smiled and linked arms with her. "First, we convince your mother, then my mother. With them on our side, our fathers will surely consent!"

"That's the plan." Rosalind smoothed her hair back. "Men are the heads of the household, but women are the hearts, and every sensible person on earth knows which of the two is stronger."

five

"Hae they gone daft?" Ewan rubbed his eyes but found no relief. "Do you see that? Tables and benches they've set up o'er near a summer kitchen?"

"I see it." Johnny didn't sound as though he disliked the sight at all.

"They're not planning on selling dinner. Surely they know better." Ewan thumped a moonstruck Johnny on the upper arm. Johnny's eyes still followed the little blond's every movement.

"I'm afraid not." Arthur's voice, heavy with misgiving, sounded behind them.

"I aim to be first in line," Johnny planned aloud, receiving glares for his enthusiastic support of the womenfolk.

"How did this come t' be?" Ewan struggled to maintain a calm demeanor. *Did I not speak wi' the man scarce three days past about keepin' the townswomen clear o' the workmen? This'll set the cats about the pigeons before I can so much as blink!*

"'Tis the honest truth, I'm not all too certain." Arthur's brow furrowed in puzzlement. "I came home to find my favorite meal on the table, and Rosey talking about how she wanted to contribute to the growth of the community, and my sweet Kaitlin sayin' as how 'twas a good opportunity for the girls to learn the value of hard work in a business setting."

"And you said 'twas a foolish idea?" Ewan felt a sort of sinking in the region of his stomach at the older man's sheepish look.

42

"I said I'd hae to think on the matter, and the next thing I knew, Kaitlin left the table and came back with a fresh rhubarb pie and the sweetest smile you ever did see." He gave a rueful grin. "The next thing I know, I'm making benches."

"Good man," Johnny approved over Ewan's groan. "If I could say so, sir, I think you made a very wise choice. Excellent."

"We'll see." Ewan tried to think positively. *Lord, is there any possibility You could make the men so distracted by good, homemade food that they'll ignore any other. . .attractions?* He glanced over to where Rosalind and—what was her name? Arleen?—spoke animatedly, creamy cheeks flushed with excitement and effort.

Lord, I can see I'm coming to the right place for help. 'Tis gonna take nothing short of a miracle.

Refusing to dwell on it, Ewan worked so single-mindedly that the morning all but flew by. He'd just set down a pair of tongs when Johnny yanked his arm and practically dragged him over to the table nearest the makeshift kitchen. Left without a choice, Ewan plunked down.

The rich, hickory smell of that pot of pork and beans doesn't tempt me in the slightest. Those steaming trays of sweet golden cornbread aren't enticing in the least. I'm here only because 'twould be rude to leave.

Ewan kept a litany of protective statements running through his mind, trying to convince himself that he wasn't pleased as punch to be the first man sitting at the table, with Rosalind smiling at him and ladling out a hearty serving of beans.

"Smells wonderful," he praised. "Such a clever idea to set up an outdoor diner where you'll have customers in droves." *Fool. And to think, I thought less of Arthur for giving his blessing. At least the man had a wife and daughter trying to convince him, and he made it all the way to dessert! I haven't even taken my first bite.*

Determined to stop himself before he said anything else, Ewan filled his mouth with pork and beans. *Mmm. Meaty, filling, slightly sweet, and perfectly cooked.* He closed his eyes and took another bite before he realized Rosalind and the other girl were watching him and Johnny expectantly.

"Good," Johnny grunted, making short work of his bowl and slathering a piece of cornbread with butter. "Best thing I've tasted in months."

The girls' faces lit up at the verdict before they turned to hear Ewan's opinion.

"Best pork 'n beans I've ever had," he admitted. Rosalind practically beamed at his compliment, and Ewan accepted the truth. When Rosalind MacLean set her mind to something, whether it be her father's permission, a thriving business, or his own grudging approval, she found a way to get it. If he wasn't so busy savoring his piece of cornbread, Ewan just might have to think about how disturbing that was. He took a second piece, just for good measure.

"Well then, I think we're ready to open." With that, the blond girl rang the dinner bell loud and clear. Hungry workers came sniffing around in hopes of some good food. They were delighted to find it in plentiful supply. Word spread quickly, and soon the benches at the table creaked with the weight of satisfied customers.

Ewan's good mood evaporated as he took stock of the hungry eyes following the girls' progress around the tables. A few watched the saucy sway of Rosalind's skirt with more interest than they showed the food she placed before them. The only thing that helped Ewan's uneasiness was the knowledge that the girls' fathers were keeping close guard on the situation.

When the men finished clearing every morsel, they exited en masse, leaving soiled tables full of dirty dishes and cornbread crumbs in their wake. Even the girls' families left without offering to pitch in. Ewan frowned to see the amount of work the girls had before them. They looked anything but upset.

"We did it!" The girls chorused as they hugged.

"We might even need to make more tomorrow, just in case the men tell a few of their friends," Rosalind added.

"Word will spread," Johnny broke in. "Tomorrow will be a mad rush to get a spot at one of your tables. You'll be turning customers away in droves before you know it."

"It'd be a good idea to have your fathers and brothers— men you trust—overseeing a table each to make sure no fights break out." *If you can't beat 'em, join 'em.* "Things could get ugly if you're not careful."

"We hadn't thought of that." The blond—Marlene, Johnny had told him—showed signs of worry on her pretty young face.

"Dustin, Da, Isaac. . . I don't think Brent is formidable enough to control a group of grown men, and Luke certainly can't. That's only three, and we have five tables." Rosalind bit her lower lip. She looked so delicate. Ewan knew he was sunk when she turned her brilliant blue eyes toward him with a speculative gleam. "Would you and Johnny consider helping us out in return for your dinner five times a week?"

"Absolutely!" Johnny grinned at Marlene. "Anything we can do to help, you just let us know. We'll take care of it."

"I'd be glad to pitch in." Ewan looked down at Rosalind. "And I'd still be more than willing to pay for your cooking. 'Tis worth far more than the asking price as is."

"You'll not pay for a meal at these tables, Mr. Gailbraith,"

Rosalind declared, unknowingly giving him a reminder that he had no right to be thinking of her as "Rosalind." She was Miss MacLean to him, and that was how things should be.

"I'll not argue the point, Miss MacLean." He gave her a polite smile. "At the moment, my stomach is far too full for me to gainsay you."

"Perfect." She clasped her hands together and turned to her friend. "Marlene, we did it. Everything worked out!"

As Ewan and Johnny walked back toward the forge, the afternoon's work stretching ahead of them, Ewan couldn't hold back one last doubt. *We'll see what happens tomorrow.*

❧

"I never thought I'd see the day when I saw the use of your mother's o'erpacking, Marlene." Rosalind set aside another clean plate. "Wi'out all these dishes, we'd be in a pickle."

"Be sure you tell her that last part." Marlene swished another one through the clean water. "It'll make her feel even better about helping convince father to agree to this venture."

"I did fear Da might take back his agreement when he saw that bunch of hungry men swarming all around our new benches." Rosalind massaged the small of her back for a leisurely moment before returning to the task at hand. "Praise the Lord all went well today. Had the slightest thing gone wrong, that would hae been the end of it."

"Well, it's only the beginning"—Marlene scrubbed a particularly stubborn splotch of dried food—"which means we have plans to make and supplies to purchase before long."

"Aye. We should start by deciding what we'll be cooking for the rest of the week." Rosalind paused to consider what would be simplest to make in vast quantities. "Maybe shepherd's pie?"

"Agreed. Why don't we make it a policy to have some kind

of soup or stew as the main dish every other day?" Marlene pushed back a few straggling locks of her golden hair. "With enough variety, the men won't complain. It's the simplest thing to make for so many. . .and hearty enough for working men."

"Let me think a moment." Rosalind ticked off types of stew and soup. "There's Irish, corn, and beef stew, and potato, parsnip, and split pea soup. . . . If we add a pork bone to Scotch broth, that will serve. Along wi' pork 'n beans, Welsh rarebit, and biscuits with gravy, we'll hae enough simple recipes to see us through."

"Exactly." Marlene rubbed her hands together in anticipation. "We'll need to stock up on all the vegetables we can buy and see about having the men slaughter another hog to keep us in provisions. We'll need cornmeal for johnnycake, flour for biscuits and bread. . . . How soon do you think we can persuade one of the menfolk to take us to the general store?"

"Soon, I hope, though we've already asked for their help at the tables every dinner. 'Tis glad I am to have enlisted the aid of Mr. Gailbraith and his friend. They'll help smooth things along."

"Johnny," Marlene murmured absently, dreamily swirling her finger in the sandy pebbles lining the brook.

"What?" Rosalind turned a gimlet eye on her friend. "When did you become familiar enough wi' the man to call him by his Christian name? Surely you hae not given him leave to address you so."

"I should say not." Marlene snapped back to attention. "He calls me Miss Freimont as is right and proper, but he invited me to call him Johnny. I haven't done so to his face," she added hastily at the warning glint in Rosalind's eyes.

"See that you don't. Mam says a young miss can't be too careful around strange men, no matter how affable they appear. Using each others' first name signifies a familiarity inappropriate between the two of you." Her warning delivered, Rosalind sank back on her heels and admitted, "Though I've had to remind myself of the same thing when I think on Mr. Gailbraith."

"Ooh!" Marlene squealed and abandoned the dishes altogether. "I knew it. I just *knew* it! You haven't so much as cast an interested glance at any other railroad worker."

"That's simply untrue." Rosalind grinned. "I gave that one man an interested glance when he claimed he owned the entire railroad."

"That's not the type of interest I'm meaning, and you know it, Rose." Marlene shook her head. "I meant the kind of interest that makes a woman's eyes widen and her knees go weak."

"Sounds to me as though such a hapless woman wouldn't withstand a terrible fright."

"You know what I mean." Marlene shot her friend an exasperated glance. "The type of feeling that makes you want to call Mr. Gailbraith by his first name."

"Rubbish." Rosalind waved the notion aside. " 'Tis only that 'Ewan' seems to suit him far better than his surname."

"And you're in a position to know such things since when? Best come out with it, Rose. You've seen the handsome blacksmith quite often since he began working near your father. Don't pretend you haven't looked forward to seeing him around and perhaps exchanging a friendly greeting."

"I—" The intended denial stuck fast in Rose's throat. *If I were to be honest, I do look forward to Ewan's—Mr. Gailbrath's—*

warm smile and cheery wave. Could his resemblance to Da while working over the forge be the only reason, or had a different sort of fondness crept into her heart over the past week?

"Aha!"

Rosalind realized her awkward pause had not escaped her friend's notice.

"I thought as much," Marlene crowed, sobering quickly when Luke popped into sight. "Luke's coming." She welcomed Luke brightly. "Come to lend a hand, have you? Well, we've plenty enough dishes to tote back and pack inside the crates." She leaned back toward Rosalind to give a whisper. "Don't think that this conversation is over, Rose!"

I was afraid of that.

six

Ewan strove mightily to attend to his work, focusing on the iron he'd heated to a glowing red and now manipulated into the proper shape. Trouble was, he couldn't help but notice Rosalind MacLean, along with Luke and their blond friend whom Johnny seemed to have taken a shine to, riding past his forge in a buckboard and then heading into the small mercantile.

'Tis early in the morning. You've no call to be letting your mind wander from your work, Ewan Gailbraith. He sternly forced himself to concentrate on the task at hand and finished reshaping the implement before cooling it in the tempering bath.

A fine job, if I do say so myself. He gave a mighty stretch and glanced toward the general store. *'Tis no quick trip for a peppermint whim. The lasses hae been in there a goodly amount of time. Perhaps they're browsing as women are apt to do.*

He looked to his next task. 'Twould take the better part of the morning to repair the broken wheel. Montana Central needed an official wheelwright to repair the wagons that carried loads of supplies away from the train cars and to the more remote areas where workers cleared the land and made ways through forest and rock. As it was, the work fell on his shoulders. He found it useful to know many skills, but he'd learned an unpleasant truth. The more kinds of work a railroad man was able to do, the more he'd be called upon to do. Whether he'd been hired on to do the task wasn't a big part of the equation.

Learning to do every scrap of work possible was how I helped support Mam after Da came to America. Any trade that involved working wi' iron, I turned a hand to.

"Ewan?" Johnny's hesitant tone caught Ewan's attention at once. Blacksmithing was good, honest work, but a simple mistake could cost a man dearly.

"Aye?" He quickly surveyed his new friend and found nothing visibly wrong. The tension in his shoulders eased.

"I'm finished with this bit." The younger man gestured toward the whorls of steam rising from the tempering bath as it cooled the heated metal within.

"Good." Ewan bit back a grin as Johnny cast a furtive glance toward the general store down the road. It appeared he wasn't the only one who'd noticed the ladies' destination this morning.

"And it occurred to me that I could use"—Johnny's brow furrowed—"an. . .er. . .well, this place could certainly use a few. . ."

"A few. . .what?" Ewan crossed his arms over his chest, delighting in his friend's awkward ploy to see the girls in the shop.

"Pounds of fresh-ground coffee!" His triumphant pronouncement made him nod sagely. "You know, to keep up our strength throughout the day. Nothin' like a pot of hot, strong coffee."

"Like this one?" Ewan hefted the pot keeping warm by the forge and made a show of peering around. "Seems as though we've a goodly enough supply to see us through the week." He put down the pot and nudged a sack with the toe of his leather boot.

"Oh." Johnny's face fell. "Right."

"Although"—Ewan decided to finally take pity on the poor fellow and give his consent—"it seems to me that you can never have too much coffee on hand. We might well invite Arthur over for a mug or two."

"Only neighborly!" Johnny untied his heavy, soot-stained leather apron and had it over his head in record time.

"I could do wi' a bit of a break, myself," Ewan admitted, pulling off his thick work gloves. *And seeing some of the pretty things on display at the store would be a welcome change.*

Together, the pair made their way to the general store.

"Good placement they've set up," Johnny noted. "Smithy's in the middle of the village, and the store's nearby, but far enough away not to catch most of the ash."

"Wi' the railroad, this place will flourish into a thriving city before too long." Ewan shrugged off a vague discomfort at the notion. This place—with its endless skies, fresh air, mountains full of good pine, and tight-knit community—wouldn't maintain all its current charm in the face of progress. The thought saddened him, even as he told himself the railroad would ensure the survival of Saddleback.

"I hope it doesn't change too much," Johnny said, unwittingly echoing Ewan's own thoughts. "I'd hate to see the place turned into one of those crowded, gritty modern cities I've seen too many of."

Ewan gave a terse nod in reply as they stepped through the mercantile doors. A welcoming coolness settled around him as he made his way further into the well-insulated shop, wending his way past farming implements, seeds, buckets, sacks, rope, and various examples of leatherwork.

"Here we go." Johnny stopped in front of the large grinder

but kept his head turned toward the back counter.

"Mr. Mathers!" The girl called Marlene greeted Johnny with a charming smile before giving Ewan a sedate nod. He didn't miss the way she nudged Rosalind with her elbow while doing so.

"Mr. Gailbraith." Rosalind's acknowledgement, while friendly, bore a hint more reserve than that of her friends.

"Miss MacLean. Miss Freimont." He took stock of the mound of merchandise dominating the counter. "I'd be happy to lend a hand."

"Thank you." Her smile deepened, and a tiny dimple flittered in her right cheek. She got prettier every day.

"Welcome," Johnny jumped in. "We wouldn't let you little ladies haul a load this big."

"I'm glad to say we won't be carrying it farther than the wagon outside," Rosalind smiled. "Though 'twas such a lovely day for a walk, we gave a thought to leaving it behind."

"Although, it is an awful lot of things, isn't it? Somehow it seems heavier when it's right in front of you than when you just write it down on a list." Miss Freimont pressed a hand to her heart. "Your help would be greatly appreciated. We remembered a few things not on our list once we got here."

"Must hae been quite a list." Ewan raised an eyebrow.

"Indeed." Rosalind pulled a piece of paper, filled with handwriting, out of her sleeve and squinted to read the tiny script. "Though I think we've all the supplies we could possibly need for the diner. Except for the vegetables." She turned to the shopkeeper. "We'll be needing to take a look at your carrots, parsnips, onions, and potatoes before we tally it all up." She headed for the large crates holding the produce.

Johnny's smile, if possible, grew wider as he dug his elbow

into Ewan's ribs. "Looks like we can count on delicious dinners for the rest of the week, at the very least! I hope they make mashed potatoes—they're my favorite." He whispered this last.

"We'll be sure to consider that, Mr. Mathers." Rosalind's promise proved Johnny's whisper had carried a bit too far.

"Of course," Miss Freimont agreed with a twinkle in her eye. "After all, we want to keep our favorite customers happy."

❧

Rosalind sucked in a shocked gasp at Marlene's blatant flirtation with the two railroad blacksmiths. Such forwardness! And yet, her disapproval was tinged with another, darker emotion she recognized as envy. *How can she be so at ease around these men?*

She relaxed when she saw a hint of rebuke in Ewan's—Mr. Gailbraith's—eyes. *So 'tis not just that I'm socially awkward. Such saucy comments are too volatile for even Mr. Gailbraith.*

"We want to make sure our cooking keeps bringing patrons to the outdoor diner, of course." Rosalind diffused the tension Marlene remained oblivious to. "And we especially appreciate your willingness to try the dishes before we open every afternoon."

"Not as much as we appreciate your fine cooking." Ewan's—Mr. Gailbraith's—smile gave a sense of warm sincerity, and Rosalind could tell he knew exactly what she'd been trying to do when she spoke up.

To cover her sudden awkwardness, she turned her attention back to her long list. "Mr. Acton, if you'd let me know what we've collected while I check it off my list, 'twould greatly ease my mind."

"Of course," Mr. Acton agreed as he added bushels of

vegetables to the order. "Vegetables, eggs, flour, cornmeal, sugar, brown sugar, baking soda, molasses, beans, a wheel of cheese, vanilla extract, cinnamon, nutmeg, salt, pepper, and coffee. Is there anything left on your list, Miss MacLean?"

"Wait a moment. . . ." She looked at all the crossed-off items one last time. "Salt pork." Rosalind glanced up to find the railroad men both looking as though the very mention of that much food caused a corresponding emptiness in their stomachs.

"If I may ask, Miss MacLean," the blacksmith ventured, "what are you planning on for today's dinner?"

"You'll hae to wait and see, Mr. Gailbraith." Rosalind shifted closer to the counter. "Though, if you had a request, what would it be?"

"After the pork 'n beans and shepherd's pie, I'd gladly tuck into any dish you set before me." His smile reached up to brighten his green eyes. "Though I must admit I bear a certain fondness for Irish stew."

"As do I, Mr. Gailbraith." She watched as the shopkeeper tallied their order.

"Seems we have a lot in common." His voice lowered so only she could hear, and the deep rumble sent a thrill down her spine. "Irish heritage, smithing families, and now favorite dishes."

"Here you are." Mr. Acton claimed her attention as she completed the transaction.

"Luke!" She called him away from the corner where he'd been admiring a few fancy toys. "We're ready to get going."

"Then let's head off." Ewan shouldered the heaviest load with manful ease. "For a man never knows what may lie ahead."

Is it my imagination, or was he looking at me as he said that? A giddy little bubble filled her heart at the idea, only to swiftly deflate as she remembered her mother's words—a woman could never be too careful with a strange man. *What lies ahead could be dangerous.*

That sobering thought cast a cloud over the beautiful day.

Lord, You hae written that You love a cheerful giver, and Ewan lends a hand without thinking about it. How can I meet his selfless generosity wi' suspicion? Return distrust for help so freely given? And yet, Your Word tells that we are to seek wise counsel. How to behave around a man so strong and good-natured as Ewan, 'tis certainly beyond my own experience. If 'tis possible to join caution wi' caring, 'tis what I must do, though I cannot see how the two align. I've not the time to dwell upon the matter just now, but 'twill be in my thoughts. I ask for the wisdom to see and follow Your will.

"Oh!" Marlene's gasp caused Rosalind's gaze to follow hers. The modest buckboard, loaded down with their many purchases, was filled to bursting. Even the narrow bench up front for the driver held one of the crates of vegetables.

" 'Tis a small matter," Rosalind assured her. "Luke may drive it ahead, and we'll follow on foot."

"And what of dinner? We haven't the time to walk for a half hour before unloading the wagon and beginning." Marlene's voice came out low and rapid. "More time has passed while we were in the store than we planned for."

"Ewan and I are glad to come along," Mr. Mathers pronounced loudly, his eyes fastened on Marlene's upset expression. "We'll unload everything."

"Thank you!" Marlene seemed all but ready to hug the man, and Rosalind swiftly linked arms with her to avoid that catastrophe.

Luke drove the buckboard back to the outdoor oven that was the hub of the diner, and the other four followed more slowly on foot.

"Oof!" Marlene suddenly lurched forward, dragging Rosalind away from her thoughts and toward the hard-packed dirt.

Rosalind jerked her arm back, attempting to compensate for Marlene's lack of balance. The maneuver was successful, and neither of them landed facedown in the dirt, though Marlene seemed to feel the incident to have been very traumatic.

"I tripped over a root, just there." Marlene pointed to a bare, even patch of earth, and Rosalind's eyes narrowed in suspicion. Marlene must have noticed, because she hastily swayed the tiniest bit to grasp hold of Mr. Mathers's arm. "Perhaps it was a rock that moved. Oh, I think I've turned my ankle." Her light lashes fluttered as though valiantly holding back tears, and Rosalind immediately regretted her uncharitable thoughts.

"Are you all right, Marlene?" She tried to loop Marlene's arm over her shoulders, but her friend pulled away and clung to Mr. Mathers instead.

"I'll be fine," she asserted a bit breathlessly as the young man slipped a supporting arm around her waist. "Yes, that's. . . better."

"I'd be glad to help you walk the rest of the way, miss." His offer couldn't have come any quicker, and he seemed loathe to let go of Marlene anytime soon—a fact Rosalind noted warily.

"How gallant of you," Marlene breathed, leaning gracefully against his stalwart support. "I'll be fine in no time at all.

Usually I'm far more nimble." She cast her gaze to Rosalind, obviously expecting her friend to back her up on this.

"Yes," Rosalind agreed drily. "By far."

"Well, if Miss Freimont is up to it"—Ewan's voice had the vaguest hint of doubt—"we'd best continue. Miss MacLean?" He politely proffered his own arm to Rosalind, as was proper.

"I think 'twould be best." She tucked her hand in the crook of his arm, feeling the warmth of his strong muscles through the thin cambric of his everyday shirt. Suddenly feeling slightly out of breath herself, she gulped in the fresh mountain air in what came out as a sort of heavy sigh.

"Don't fret," Ewan patted her hand comfortingly. "Your wee little friend will be fine, of that I bear no doubt at all."

"Of course," she murmured, looking at the couple slowly making their way before them. Although Marlene leaned against the support Mr. Mathers so readily offered, her step showed no sign of an injured ankle.

Rosalind bit back a comment.

"To my way of thinking," Ewan said, his deep rumble soothing her ire, " 'tis simply an example of something I was taught long ago."

"Oh?" Rosalind quirked a brow, wondering what wisdom the handsome blacksmith would share with her. *A man like Ewan Gailbraith must know all sorts of things I wouldn't.*

"Sometimes," he bent his head closer to hers and spoke with a conspiratorial grin, "when it serves a purpose, people seem worse than they truly are."

seven

Ewan hefted a bag of flour into the old smokehouse the girls were using for storage. When he returned for another load, he was caught by the sight of Rosalind as she untied her sunbonnet and drew it off.

A soft breeze tickled the springy tendrils around her face while her hair caught the sun's light and burned with a brightness bold enough to warm a man's heart. He quelled a surge of disappointment when she dutifully donned the bonnet once more to conceal her crowning glory and protect her fair skin.

Lord, You truly hae made everything beautiful in Your time. 'Tis struck I am to see the loving stroke of Your hand around me, and the bearer of Your stamp so unaware o' it. Beauty is one thing; beauty wi'out the stain of pride gives even more pleasure.

"Are you certain?" Johnny, eagerly bringing Miss Freimont some cool water, sounded genuinely anxious. *Young pup.*

"Certainly." Marlene pointed the dainty toe of her boot downward, then flexed it upward, causing the frills of her petticoat to froth over her ankle in a flagrantly feminine display. It worked, too. Johnny watched the motion, transfixed.

Ewan rolled his eyes. *If I didn't know any better, I'd say the minx had "tripped" on purpose to garner more attention. But surely no woman would use such an obvious ploy. . . .* He saw her laughing charmingly at something or other a besotted Johnny had said. The girl certainly had her eye on the lad. *Would she?*

59

He carried more sacks to the converted smokehouse, after taking a moment to clear his head. When he got back to the unloading, Ewan practically bumped into Rosalind as she came out of the tiny structure. Ewan quickly stepped back getting a firmer grip on the goods he held lest they topple upon her pretty little head.

She gave him a ghost of a smile and sidestepped, obviously concerned with getting the work done in time to begin dinner. The tip of her braid bounced against the slim curve of her back as she walked the few steps to the wagon and reached up.

Now, there is a woman who wouldn't need to resort to petty wiles to catch a man's attention. She carries herself like a lady.

And she was carrying another sack back toward him. While she'd continued working, he'd stood and stared like an imbecile. Ewan swiftly deposited his load and strode past her to gather the last of the items. He cast an irritated glance to where Johnny still paid court to no-longer-maimed-but-not-helping Marlene.

"Oh, no." He felt Rosalind's small hand press against his forearm where he'd rolled up his sleeves at the same time he heard her sweet, clear voice.

He almost dropped what he carried. "What's wrong?" He craned his neck to look down at her upturned face. Ewan watched in fascination as her cornflower blue eyes widened and her mouth opened in surprise at the unexpected intimacy of the moment before she yanked her hand back as though the brief contact had scalded her as it had him.

"I—I put those things aside so we could use them today." She looked toward the summer kitchen. "They need to go over there."

"Fine, then." He smiled, then looked at the bounty in his arms as his stride covered the short distance. Among other things, he held a modest crate filled with potatoes, onions, and carrots. A small sack held some precious spices, most likely salt and pepper. He cast a glance over his shoulder to see her exiting the old smokehouse with a piece of meat. He squinted to see it—lamb.

She's making Irish stew, just like I asked. The realization flooded him with unexpected warmth. *Pretty Rosalind wi' the dancing braid and twinkling eyes wants to show her thanks for our help, and she found a circumspect way to do it. Aye, the lass is every inch a lady.*

Yes, he'd do well to keep a watch over Rosalind MacLean—and it wouldn't be a hardship to do so.

❧

"Don't worry!" Rosalind turned Marlene away from where she stood staring at what seemed an impossible apple harvest.

Bushel upon bushel of the fruits filled the barn, emptied of its usual occupants to make room for this new purpose. Tart, yellow-green apples sat apart from their sweeter, deep red cousins, the bounty almost overwhelming.

All right, Lord. Truth be told, 'tis overwhelming. Every year the apple trees Delana brought here yield more and more fruit. Give us hearts grateful for Your provision, rather than thoughts of aching shoulders.

"This will take days!" Marlene frowned. "We'll have to shut down the diner."

With a pang, Rosalind realized she wouldn't see Ewan—*Mr. Gailbraith, Mr. Gailbraith, Mr. Gailbraith*, she reminded herself harshly—until Sunday meeting. Which was, if she recalled rightly, to be held in this very barn.

Can we finish the work wi' only Mam, Delana, Marlene, Grandmam, Mrs. Parkinson, and the Twadley girls? She stared at the abundance of apples once more. *Surely not. And the men work at harvesting this time of year. 'Twas good of them to help pick the apples!* Rosalind sighed.

"I've an idea." Marlene whirled around giddily. "I'd warrant we could get the men to do it."

"Marlene! Your father, brother, and uncle hae more than enough to do in the fields. And Da works all the day long, too. We'll not shirk our fair share."

"So serious, Rose!" Marlene giggled. "I meant the men who come to our diner. What if we announced an apple bee? We'll have music and laughter and some supper to make the time go by."

" 'Twould be doable if we were to double whatever we make for dinner." Rosalind thought about it. "And to sweeten the deal, we could promise them apple cobbler wi' dinner later in the week."

"Now you're thinking!" Marlene scanned the open working space in the barn. "We'll bring in the benches for folks to sit on and our tables to hold the food. Mr. Twadley will bring his fiddle, and Luke's a whiz at playing the spoons. Brent would like the chance to show off with his harmonica."

"We'll hae an apple paring contest wi' the prize to be a fresh apple pie the next day." Rosalind thought of how best to make sure the work got done. "The men can take the pared apples to the cider press afterward. If enough men show up for the bee, we can get most of the work done in one evening!"

"Oh," Marlene spoke smugly, "they'll come. Just you wait and see. Tomorrow night, there won't be room enough for all the men who want to help."

The next afternoon, all the women of the town came from miles around to lend a hand. Soon, the wooden tables groaned under loaves of bread, pans of johnnycake, plates of biscuits, crocks of butter, platters of chicken, and two massive pots of Marlene and Rosalind's thick, creamy potato soup.

The diner benches lined the working area, with buckets and crates placed everywhere for the apple peels. Every hog in town would be well fed. Paring knives lay in rows; thick, brown string waited to hold apple slices for drying; and the cider press stood ready a short distance from the barn. Barrels next to heaps of straw were ready to cold-pack the fruit destined for the root cellars.

The men would come straight after the workday, and they'd work by lantern light until eyes drooped. With the barn doors thrown wide open, they'd carefully placed lanterns so as not to risk a fire.

The women took their places by the doors, closest to the waiting apples, as the men trickled in. Rosalind marveled at the difference in how they worked.

The women deftly turned their apples, sliding the paring blade smoothly beneath the skin to slick off the peel in one long rind of curlicues. The men attacked the apples as though whittling, moving the knives in short jerks to send shaved bits of peel flying into the buckets.

"I once heard," one of the Twadley girls confided to Rosalind and Marlene, "that if you peel the whole skin into one strip and toss it behind you, whatever shape the peel falls into on the floor represents the name of the man you'll marry!"

"What fun!" Marlene's hands moved with more cautious

determination as she worked, though she kept her gaze fixed firmly on the men entering the barn. When Marlene straightened, her hands going still for the barest moment, Rosalind looked to the doorway.

There, his powerful frame gilded by the lantern light, stood Ewan. His broad shoulders all but blocked the smaller man who stood at his side.

Rosalind felt her breath hitch as Ewan stepped farther inside, his gaze passing over the barn's occupants and coming to rest on her. He dipped his head in acknowledgement before walking over to take a seat next to her father.

Mr. Mathers, much to Marlene's delight, made a beeline toward her. She none too subtly scooted over to make room for him to plunk down, leaving Rosalind clinging to the edge of the bench.

Discomfited and not eager to examine why, Rosalind put down her knife and the apple she'd just finished paring. She dropped the long peel into the bucket behind her as she left for a drink of water.

Marlene's hastily smothered gasp made her turn around. There, obviously having missed the bucket, sat Rosalind's long apple peel, its curls resolutely shaped into an unmistakable letter *E*.

eight

"For pity's sake, Johnny." Ewan laid down his hammer as he caught his assistant giving him yet another odd look. "If you hae something to say, come out wi' it already."

"I— Oh, nothing." Johnny turned his back to Ewan.

"We're men. Quit shilly-shallying about and looking at me as though I've grown a second nose or sommat equally interesting. You're twitching more than a horse wi' pesky flies. 'Tis distracting."

"What do you think of Miss MacLean?" The younger man now wore a cautious, crafty expression Ewan found to be even more off-putting than the furtive glances.

"She's a fine lass." Ewan shrugged and said no more. *Pretty as a fiery sunset spreading o'er a blue sky, God-fearing, hardworking, deeply loyal, intelligent, kind. . . The list goes on. I won't be telling any o' that to Johnny, though.*

"I see." Johnny sounded more subdued, disappointed even. "It's just that Marlene told me that she—Miss MacLean, that is—she got a sign last night at the apple bee. And—"

"Johnny!" Ewan bit out the name. "You're clucking like a gossipy hen, you know that?" *I don't want to hear about Rosalind getting a love-token from some other man. She deserves better than the fellows I've seen hereabouts, and that's that.*

"Fine." He sounded a bit huffy as he tossed a few last words over his shoulder. "If you don't want to know that she returns your high opinion of her but is too proper to say so. . ."

65

Ewan froze as Johnny's voice trailed off, tantalizing him with the thought that Rosalind might have noticed him the way he'd noticed her—the way he'd kept noticing her since the very first time they met.

"Oh?" He struggled to keep his tone neutral as he sought more information, but Johnny gave a shrug and said no more. "And this is leading to what?" he finally prompted more explicitly.

"Surely you don't expect *me* to say anything." Johnny inspected a piece of iron, obviously decided it wasn't ready, and thrust it back into the forge. "I don't want to sound like a. . .what was it?" His brow furrowed as he repeated, "A gossipy hen, right?"

"I may hae been a wee bit hasty," Ewan admitted grudgingly.

"I'm glad to hear you realize that." Johnny, his lips firmly set, refrained from saying anything more. His silence was deafening.

"Johnny!" Ewan roared at long last. "Just tell me whatever 'tis that seemed so important naught but five minutes ago!"

"Marlene is of the opinion that Miss MacLean thinks highly of you." Johnny stretched to get the cricks out of his muscles. "More highly of you than any of the men who've been sniffing around her lately. Marlene reckons her best friend has eyes for you, Ewan. I aimed to see if you returned her interest."

"Aye," Ewan admitted aloud for the first time. "She's a rare woman. But I'd hae no thought of courting her, you see."

"No, I don't see." Johnny gaped at him. "A pretty young lady who cooks like an angel and seems to like you above other men, and you have no thought of seeking her out? You're daft!"

"Now, Johnny—" Ewan stopped his protest before he uttered it. *Maybe he's right. How long hae I been thinking about settling down? And here the Lord brings me to the MacLean doorstep, where beautiful Rosalind is ripe for marriage.* "That may bear thinking on."

"Too right, it does." Johnny picked up his tongs once more. "I've already decided to speak with Marlene's father. Come spring, I'll have enough seed money to start my own spread. And in a year, I'll have a threshold to carry my bride over."

"You don't think you're being a bit hasty?" Ewan chose his words carefully, aware of the strength of Johnny's infatuation.

"I just said we'd wait a year before Marlene and I will wed."

"So you plan to settle down and want to see others do the same, eh?" Ewan couldn't resist teasing his friend just a mite.

"Something like that. You'd make a good neighbor, and Marlene wants to stay close to her friend." Johnny picked up his hammer. "Could work out to be a real good setup."

"Could be."

Ewan mulled over the information for hours, praying for guidance before feeling he had made the right decision. He strode over to Arthur's forge and waited until the older man finished what he was working on before he approached.

"Ewan!" Arthur drew off his gloves and apron, smiling in welcome. "What can I do for you?" He gestured for him to sit.

"You can give me permission to call on your daughter." Ewan figured Arthur was the sort of man who'd appreciate directness.

"I wondered when it would come to that." Arthur rested his heavy hands on his knees and closed his eyes. Even after a short acquaintance with him, Ewan knew him to be praying. He waited, respecting the man's need to seek God's will even as Ewan had before coming.

He's about to ask what my intentions are toward his daughter.
Ewan straightened his shoulders and prepared to answer the question asked of would-be suitors by protective papas all the world over. He'd come with a ready answer to that.

"When you look at my Rosey," Arthur spoke slowly, drawing out the question to show its significance, "what do you see?"

Ewan paused to consider the unexpected question. He knew Arthur placed a great deal of importance on his reply, so he weighed his words carefully. There were as many ways to answer as there were things to appreciate about Rosalind herself.

"The first thing I saw was her beauty," he began honestly. " 'Twas why I spoke wi' you regarding her safety." At Arthur's nod of recollection, Ewan kept on. "Now, when I look upon her, I see a woman of warmth and integrity—a woman whose strength of character and generous heart I cannot help but admire. Her dedication to you and the rest of your family speaks well of her raising, and she carries herself as a God-fearing woman. She doesn't shirk from her duties, and I've yet to see her lose patience. In short," Ewan finished, admitting his hopes aloud for the first time, "when I look at your daughter, I see the woman I hope to share my life wi'."

He waited as Arthur thought over his response. *Did I say too little? Too much? Should I not hae mentioned her beauty? No, 'twould hae been dishonest and an obvious omission. Lord, when did feelings for Rosalind change my heart and priorities? Now everything seems to rest on this one conversation.*

"I'm well pleased wi' your answer, Ewan." Arthur gave an approving nod. "You see the beauty of her spirit and her worth beyond a pretty face and strong back. That's more than I can say for many a man hereabouts." He paused a moment. "You may court my Rosey, provided you agree to a few conditions."

Ewan waited to hear the conditions before he agreed.

"Should she reject your suit, you'll respect her decision. Should she accept it, you'll be treating her wi' the propriety an unmarried lady deserves at all times." Arthur's gaze bore into Ewan fiercely as he laid down his edicts, immovable as a wall of stone. "Her reputation will not be shadowed in any way."

"Done." Ewan reached out to shake his hand, but Arthur stopped him, holding up a cautionary palm before speaking.

"And before you speak wi' my daughter, we'll pray together. 'Tis no small thing, and we'll seek God's blessing afore all else." Arthur's expression turned wistful. "Should you win her heart and hand, it may well be I'll not see my daughter often."

This last thought hit Ewan with the force of a fist to the stomach. *He thinks I'll take her far away. Is that what marriage to her would mean, Lord? Dividing a loving family? I hae sworn never to separate kin—and I will not change my mind on the matter. Guide me, Father, that I not inflict such pain, as I hae suffered, on the family of the woman I hope to make my bride. And what if it comes down to marriage or her family, Lord? I'll not place her in that situation. Your eyes see ways I've no way of finding on my own. Help me trust You to see things through as You will, for the benefit of us both.*

❧

"Look to your hair." Marlene's quick whisper caused Rosalind to glance over her shoulder.

"Why are Da and Ewan coming so soon?" She frowned in

puzzlement. "Dinner is not near ready so early." Her breath caught in her throat as the icy hand of fear squeezed her heart in a suffocating grip. "Luke—he's unwell." Rosalind began to untie her apron strings as she hurried toward the approaching men, only to have Marlene snatch the strings and yank her backward.

"Calm yourself!" Marlene shook her head in exasperation. "Why would Mr. Gailbraith be coming with your father to tell you such a thing? And why would your father not be running to seek your aid? They're not coming here to discuss your little brother." She gave Rosalind a knowing look. "They want to talk about you. . .and Mr. Gailbraith."

"Me and. . ." The iciness subsided, replaced by a pooling warmth. Marlene had always known more about these things than she did. "You think he's asked Da to come courting me?"

"Yes. Now duck as though to check the fire, and smooth your hair and pinch your cheeks so you look your best." Marlene rolled her eyes. "You should have guessed it long ago—the way he looks at you as though he'll tear any man apart who so much as casts you a friendly smile. Why do you think his table is always so calm at lunch? He scowls with a possessive gleam. I'm only surprised he didn't speak with you before he sought your father's official approval. Johnny's already talked to me, and we're agreed he'll speak to Father after next meeting."

Rosalind stopped fussing with her hair to stare at her friend. "Johnny spoke wi' you first? 'Tisn't it proper to go to the girl's father afore making any type of declaration at all?"

"No, silly." Marlene shrugged. "The man speaks with the girl, if he has any consideration at all, and then speaks to her father as though it's the first time he dared say anything.

It appeases a father's pride and paves the way for family approval."

"But Ewan never said a word to me." Rosalind frowned. *'Tis his fault I'm caught so unaware! He's made this awkward by speaking wi' Da afore giving me so much as an inkling. Himph. Marlene knows how 'tis done, and obviously Johnny does as well. Why am I to be blindsided in this ridiculous fashion?*

"Marlene, may I borrow Rosalind for a moment?" Da's question sounded ominously formal as he pasted a smile on his face.

"Of course, Mr. MacLean." Marlene turned to the oven.

"Let us go walk to the shade of that tree." Da pointed with one hand as he offered her the crook of his arm.

Rosalind accepted it, trying to avoid Ewan's intense gaze as the three of them walked a distance from where Marlene stood. When they came to a halt, Da squeezed her hand tenderly.

"Rosey-mine, there comes a time when a father looks for his wee lassie and finds instead a lovely young lady. Perhaps she's a lovely young lady who has caught the eye of a bachelor." He gestured for Ewan to come closer. "Ewan hae properly sought my blessing afore coming to call, and I've gladly granted him permission to court you. Provided, that is, you are willing to receive his interest." His grip tightened, as though letting her know he'd enforce her decision either way.

"I see." Gratitude for Da's unconditional support welled within her. *He approves of Ewan, and that's reason enough to accept, even if he didn't hae a ready smile and a kind heart.*

She looked up to see the cautious hope flickering in his sea-green eyes and knew her answer. "I'm willing, Da."

The grin breaking out across Ewan's face urged a smile in

return as Da put her hand in Ewan's.

"I'll be leaving you two to speak for a short while then." He smiled and turned to walk back to where Marlene chopped potatoes. "Just a short while, mind!" he called over his shoulder, then left them in silence.

"Rosalind—" Ewan began. He didn't get far, as Rosalind checked to see if Da was watching, saw he wasn't, and lightly smacked Ewan's hand away. "What—"

"Listen to me, Ewan Gailbraith," she directed as she put her hands on her hips. "I'm willing to hae you pay me court and am flattered as well I should be, but 'tis a wee disgruntled I am, too, and that's a fact."

She shook a finger at his befuddled expression. "Don't look as though you don't ken what I mean. 'Twouldn't hae been overly difficult to give me some forewarning as to your intentions. I do not like to be caught unawares by anything, much less something of such importance." She finished speaking and waited for his reply. He had to understand straight from the start that he shouldn't be making such decisions without at least speaking to her first!

"I like hearing you say my name" was all he said.

"I—Did you not hear what else I said?" Rosalind demanded. " 'Tis vital you understand that I will not hae a husband who makes decisions first and speaks wi' me about them after the fact."

"Aye, Rosalind," he said, rumbling her name as though it were a blessing. "I should hae asked you first so as not to make things awkward for you." He took her hand in his once more, rubbing his thumb along her palm. "I value your thoughts and will seek them often. Does that put your mind at ease?"

No. If anything, my heart is beating fit to burst.

"Aye, that it does." She stepped slightly closer. "And 'tis honored I'll be to hae you come calling on me. . .Ewan."

nine

Ewan stared at where the heaping mound of corn ears took up even more space than the apples had not too long ago. And folks were pulling up wagonloads outside to replenish the pile as it diminished throughout the night.

"Good evening," he greeted Rosalind as he moved to sit beside her.

"Good evening," she replied. "At least, 'twill be a good night for me, I'm thinking." Her smile held a hint of mischief.

"Because we'll spend it together?" That's what made it a good evening to him, after all—sitting close enough to catch the light, fresh scent of roses her hair always carried.

"No. Well, that, too," she amended when she saw his chagrin. "I aim to beat you in the shucking competition. My two crates will be the first filled, I promise you." Her blue eyes sparkled in lighthearted challenge, needling him to answer it.

"Wi' these wee little hands?" He made a show of holding one of her dainty hands between his two large, rough ones. "'Twill take you twice as long to do half the work, though 'tis certain I am you'll put forth a grand effort."

Ewan didn't release her hand until she pulled slightly away. Then she surprised him by pressing her soft palm against his calloused one, stretching her fingers as far as they'd go. They both looked at the contrast silently for a moment. His sun-darkened skin and broad digits dwarfed her creamy delicacy.

"Well"—Rosalind's soft voice sounded slightly breathless as she turned her gaze to meet his—"there you hae it. 'Tis plain as the very nose on your face that I'll be the swifter betwixt us." Her hand exerted a slight, warm pressure against his as though to push him into agreement with her misguided boasting.

"Nay." His fingers curled over hers as he shook his head. "There is no arguing wi' what your eyes surely tell you, lass."

"Of course, which is why I'll win." She drew her hand away and lifted her chin. "My hands are small and light, so I'll be able to move more quickly than your large fingers can manage."

"We'll see." Ewan waited for Dustin Freimont to welcome everyone to the corn husking and ask God's blessing on the night's work. He tensed, ready to spring into action as the man officially began the competition.

Ewan dove into the work with determined zeal, scarcely sparing a glance at Rosalind's progress. That brief glance was enough to still his hands for a moment as he watched her swift, confident motions add another shucked ear to her already too-full crate. *How did she do that?*

He redoubled his efforts, loathe to let her best him after he'd bragged so certainly of his victory. Husks flew through the air and littered the floor in front of them as he increased his frantic pace. Ewan froze in disbelief as Rosalind stood up, signaling that her crates were completely filled. She'd not only defeated him in their private challenge, she'd bested absolutely everyone hard at work inside the walls of the barn!

She walked up to Dustin and claimed her prize—a finely sewn quilt decorated with colored scraps fashioned into an intricate pattern of interlocking rings. She exclaimed over it, causing an old woman in the far corner to beam with delight

"How did you manage that?" he whispered after she sat at his side once more. "Will you share the trick you use?"

"Ewan Gailbraith!" Rosalind scowled at him in mock disappointment. "How could you think I've any sort of trick? 'Tis plain hard work and"—she grinned in victory as she flexed her fingers in a silent display—"skill."

"I see I've underestimated you, Rosalind." He leaned close and whispered so only she could hear his next words. "You can be sure that I'll not be making the same mistake next time."

Her pink blush was all the victory he needed as they set back to work. Ewan's grin only faded when a shadow fell across him and he looked up to find a familiar young man standing before Rosalind, legs splayed, jaw set belligerently. He remembered the slight young fellow as Marlene's older brother but had an inkling he'd be remembering him differently soon.

"Rose," the youth addressed her with maddening informality, and Ewan had to remind himself that they'd probably grown up together, and thus it was an appropriate address. "Why don't you come over and sit with Marlene and myself?" He extended his hand to her, overconfident that she'd take him up on the offer.

"Brent, I'm quite comfortable here." Rosalind spoke kindly but firmly enough that the lad should have accepted her words.

"Rose"— Brent leaned closer and spoke in a low tone that carried plain as day—"you needn't feel obligated to sit near strangers out of a misplaced sense of politeness. Come sit with me and mine, where you belong." *Now.* This last wasn't said aloud, but came across as strongly as if it had been trumpeted.

Ewan got to his feet, unwilling to let the stripling order his Rosalind about or attempt to stake a claim to her affection.

He needn't have made the effort. Rosalind fixed Brent with an outraged stare and crossed her arms as a further barrier.

"Brent Freimont, 'tis not your place to decide where I belong. And 'tis angered I am to hear you label me as one of *yours*, as though I were a prize sow displayed at the fair."

Realizing his error too late, Brent stammered an apology.

"I appreciated your kind invitation, Brent"—Rosalind gentled her scowl but kept her tone disapproving—"but when I politely expressed disinterest, you should have behaved like a gentleman and respected my decision rather than try to force your way."

"Yes, Rose." The boy made a swift bow and retreated back to where the rest of his family sat, obviously watching them all with an avid curiosity—and a hint of apprehension, as well.

Ewan returned his focus to where it belonged—Rosalind. She looked up at him, half chagrined over the scene, half defying him to question the way she'd handled the issue.

He sat beside her, moving as close as was decent, and gave voice to his opinion. "It seems as though I'm not the only one to underestimate you, Rosalind." He fingered the silken end of her braid to show support. "I'm only glad I'll have the chance to rectify that."

❧

Men. Rosalind viciously ripped off another corn husk and threw it down before reaching for the next one. *Bad enough that Ewan discomfits me so, but to hae Brent saunter up and try to stake a claim as though I hae no say in the matter. . . Ugh. Incredible!*

"Which do you prefer, the apple bee or the corn shucking?" Ewan's question broke through her thoughts as though he knew what she was thinking. He waited patiently for her answer.

"Neither." Rose gave in to the contrary mood. "My favorite gathering is the sugaring-off. 'Tis the most fun and tasty."

"Sugaring-off? I'd the notion 'twas only done in Vermont or such."

"No, we've sugar maples here, as well." Rose took a shallow breath. "We don't harvest the sap until February. I suppose the railroad will hae moved on long before that." It was as close as she could come to asking what he planned for the future.

Will he continue to work for the rail lines, and take me wi' him to see all America? Excitement surged at the idea, even as her heart sank. *Could I leave Mam and Da and Luke behind if I knew 'twould be forever?*

Intent upon harvesting some clue from Ewan's answer, she peeked at his face from the corner of her eye. They both continued divesting ears of corn of their husks.

"Aye." The single syllable came out forced, and Rosalind saw a shadow pass over his countenance. He said no more, and she did not press the matter.

Lord, I've always wanted to travel the length and breadth of the nation. All the same, I yearned for that adventure with certain knowledge of everyone here waiting to welcome my return. I always thought to settle nearby when I finally wed. It never occurred to me that the man I marry might hae different ideas. Now 'tis far too soon to press Ewan about the matter, but 'twill have to be addressed sometime. Give me the wisdom to handle my doubts and find peace in the path You place before me.

"Rosalind?" Ewan rose to his feet. "Would you fancy a drink o' water?" He gestured toward the large bucket.

"Aye." She smiled her thanks, relieved to see no sign of the shadow from earlier. He behaved as an attentive suitor should and now 'twas the time to take note of such fine qualities. No sense borrowing trouble, as Da would say.

She reached for another ear and peeled back some of the crisp green cover. A flash of deep red peeked out, and she covered it immediately.

Oh, no! She could feel herself flushing a shade to rival the red corn. *I'll not kiss Ewan in front of the whole town! He'll be back in a moment.*

She looked about for Marlene. Rosalind had passed any red ears to her bolder best friend for years now. But Marlene sat next to Johnny—and Brent—across the way. *Oh, bother.*

As Ewan shouldered his way back into view, Rosalind debated what to do. Would she dare slip the red ear into his pile? No. 'Twould still mean sharing their first kiss before everyone she ever knew. As Ewan stopped to say something to a man she didn't recognize, Rosalind dropped the ear and kicked it under the bench behind her skirts.

Ewan gave her an odd look as he handed her a tin of water, and she hastily gulped some to cover her unease. She smiled brightly and patted the bench beside her. Rosalind breathed a tiny sigh of relief as he settled onto the seat and began to share stories from his years working for the railroad.

"Now, I'll not be telling you all these are true, but men in the railroad camps hae been swapping stories for years. Some o' the tales sound reasonable enough to keep telling."

"Do you know any funny stories?" Rosalind asked. "I've heard about the wrecks, and those make me sad."

"Nay." Ewan shook his head. "Those are warnings, not tales to be shared when a man sits beside a pretty lass."

His smile made her flush once again.

"I'll tell you a legend about one spendthrift builder and the clever foreman who outwitted him."

"That sounds good." She straightened. "Let's hear it."

"There was a builder named Mr. Hill, who kept a tight fist around the finances." Ewan's own fist tightened around the hapless ear of corn he'd just finished shucking. "He disapproved mightily of anything that could be seen as at all wasteful. Well, one day he was walking along the tracks, inspecting the work, and he spotted something in the dirt. Sure enough, he'd found a new rail spike lying deserted in the roadbed. Outraged, he stomped off to take the section foreman to task for such carelessness. They didn't have spikes to throw away."

"What a horrible man." Rosalind shuddered. "I'd hate to be that poor foreman, having to answer to that. What happened to him?"

"The quick-thinking foreman saw him coming, spotted the spike, and rushed to meet the builder. He hurries up to the man, stands tall, and says, 'Thank goodness you found that spike, Mr. Hill. I've had three men looking for it for nearly a week!'"

Rosalind burst out laughing, only speaking when she finally caught her breath. "Oh, that's a good one. Should have taught that Mr. Hill a lesson. I'd like to think that really happened."

"Me, too." Ewan chuckled. "Can't you just picture the builder's expression? He probably gaped like a caught fish."

"Most likely," Rosalind agreed. "Tell another one, please! Out here we so rarely hear things like that. We just get news."

"Hmm." Ewan thought for a moment. "I could hae another story or so to coax a smile. 'Tis a grand reward for so little."

"Flatterer." Rosalind waggled a finger at him. "Fewer fulsome compliments and more humorous stories. I enjoy those more."

"All right." He took a moment, looking as though he

enjoyed holding her interest. "Out in California, a railroad agent once got yelled at over doing things wi'out waiting for his orders to trickle down from faraway headquarters, as he should hae done. Then came a day, not long after, when the boss at headquarters received an urgent telegram from that selfsame agent: 'Grizzly bear on platform hugging conductor. Please wire instructions.'"

"No!" Rosalind's hands stilled as she looked up in shock. "Never tell me he waited afore helping that poor conductor!"

"I'm sure he took care of it before he ever sent the telegram," Ewan soothed. "The man was just trying to make a point. If he waited for official orders before doing everything, nothing would ever get done in time to do good."

"Well, in that case. . ." Rosalind relaxed. "If he kept his job, 'twas a rather clever way to argue his side of the matter."

"Aye, that's my thought, too." Ewan reached back for a mighty stretch and Rosalind, slightly more cautious since finding a red ear, peeled back a small section of husk as a safeguard.

Another gash of red blazed forth, and she hurriedly reached for another. As she grasped another ear, she let the red one roll off her lap. As before, she inconspicuously kicked it beneath the bench. Only this time, she kicked too hard. At the *thud* of the ear hitting the barn wall, Ewan looked back at her.

"What was that?" He looked around for the sound's source.

"Nothing." The word came out sounding as flustered as she felt. "You know, I'm starting to get a bit peckish." She hopped up. "Would you like me to fetch you an apple while I'm up?"

"Aye," he looked at her strangely. "A green one, please."

With a too-bright smile, she headed for the tables, selected two shiny apples, and went back. Before sitting on the bench, she looked down. It wouldn't do to slip on one of those pesky red ears she'd let drop. Wouldn't do at all.

There were no ears on the floor. Startled, she glanced up at a beaming Ewan. In each of his upraised hands lay one of the red ears.

&

"Oooh!" A swell of raucous calls filled Ewan's senses as people took note of the two ears he held up for all to see.

"Who's your lucky lady, Gailbraith?" one of the men called out. "Let her know now so she can run away!"

"I know who he'll choose!" Johnny bellowed. Beside him, Marlene was beaming and casting Rosalind knowing looks.

Rosalind, for her part, had turned as petal pink as her namesake flower and sat down as though her knees had given out. She couldn't have looked any more enticing had she tried.

Though he thought it impossible, Ewan's grin widened. *I knew I saw her hiding something behind her skirts.* Sure enough, when she'd gone to fetch the apples, he'd found two partly-unhusked ears of corn. Red ears. The thought of her squirreling away kisses charmed him. His Rosalind wouldn't hold up the red ear in triumph and boldly claim her forfeit. Instead, she clumsily hid the evidence.

Good thing I'm not shy. Ewan clasped Rosalind's hand and purposefully drew her to her feet. Her eyes, impossibly wide, shone with a beguiling mix of anxiety and anticipation.

"There's only one woman I've eyes"—Ewan waved one of the cobs of corn—"or ears for." Resisting the urge to hold her close, Ewan kept her hand in his and leaned forward to press a chaste kiss on her soft lips. After the barest moment—a moment far too short, to his way of thinking—he drew back.

Amid the stares and cheers of the crowd, Rosalind held his gaze and raised her hand to gently touch her lips. The gesture nearly made Ewan reach for her again, but he saw the moment when she remembered the whole town watched her reaction.

Ewan addressed the crowd, diverting their attention from Rosalind as best he could. " 'Tis the truth, no man could ask for more than that." He held up the second red ear and pretended to consider it. "Now then, since I've experienced perfection, 'twould be churlish of me to deny another the same opportunity."

At his words, it seemed as though every man in the barn stood and shouted to be chosen. Ewan made a show of considering whom he'd pass the second red ear to before tossing it to Johnny. Envious groans shook the barn clear to the rafters.

As though I'd give it to some other man who'd choose my Rosalind. And honestly, any other man would be daft to choose another girl. Johnny, enamored of Marlene as he is, was the only safe choice.

And Johnny made the most of his good fortune, bussing Marlene with more enthusiasm than grace. With everyone's attention turned to the other couple, Ewan and Rosalind sank back onto their bench. Their moment of excitement had ended.

"Thief." Rosalind whispered the indictment under her breath and out of the corner of her mouth. All the same, her eyes held no matching reproach to make him regret taking action.

"Sneak," Ewan muttered back, grinning at her resulting gasp.

Long seconds stretched between them before she answered. "Aye," she admitted, biting back an impish smile.

"Aye." Ewan shouldered a bit closer, beginning to regret his gift to Johnny. "You know what that makes the two of us?"

"What?" The question in her eyes seemed less lighthearted.

"It makes us"—Ewan spoke seriously, to let her know he meant what he said—"a likely pair."

ten

"Is it true that the railroad will be moving on soon?" Marlene burst out with the question almost the instant Ewan and Johnny sat down for their pre-dinner-rush meal. "You've not even been here a month! Surely this type of haste isn't typical?"

Although Rosalind wouldn't have chosen to handle the issue in this manner, she shared Marlene's worries about whether the railroad would take their beaus away with it. She looked at Ewan, careful to school her features into a neutral expression. Whatever his decision—whether he stayed for winter or left now with plans of returning later—she planned on supporting it.

"Yes, sugar-pie." Johnny looked every bit as miserable as Marlene at the prospect of leaving. "We've lingered a bit long to enjoy the comforts of home-cooking and pretty smiles, so the foreman tells us we won't be able to delay any longer. Camp will be moved a good thirty miles away. We've no choice."

"Thirty miles!" Marlene sank down onto the nearest bench, tears dotting her pale eyelashes. "Can't they at least hold off until after Thanksgiving? That's only a few days away!"

"They say they won't risk losing our impressive pace." Ewan shook his head. "Though 'tis bound to slow. Tomorrow we head out."

"Why didn't they give us a warning?" Rosalind's firm resolve not to complain melted in the face of such an immediate separation. She bit her lip.

" 'Tis for the best." Ewan rolled his massive shoulders in a vain effort to relieve tension. "If they told the men ahead of time, they'd be prone to acting out. No man wants to go back to Hank's cooking in the midst of an empty wilderness— especially wi' winter coming. This late notice, 'tis a safeguard for all the town."

"But no safeguard against heartache." Marlene's whisper probably reached only Rosalind's ears, but she decided to take no chances Ewan would overhear such maudlin dramatics.

"Marlene, we've everything ready for the men. Why don't we leave off ringing the dinner bell just a wee little bit? The news has caught us all by surprise, and 'twould do us good to spend a few private moments together." She reached out to clasp Ewan's hand. "Why don't we walk a short distance afore dinner?"

"Aye," Ewan assented.

Marlene and Johnny didn't even follow, lost as they were in one another.

After walking only a short distance, Ewan began, "Rosalind, 'tis sorry I am this matter has come upon us so sudden. 'Tis said the men took such great cheer from your diner they laid track more quickly than was expected—too much of a good thing."

" 'Tisn't as though we thought the railroad would hole up here forever," Rosalind said, "but we did think 'twould be a bit longer before you packed up and moved away from us."

"As did I." Ewan put his hands on her shoulders. "I'd not intended to hae you make any sort of decision this quickly."

Surely he wouldn't propose now. Ewan wouldn't expect me to marry and leave my family wi' such haste! I can't!

"Ewan"—Rosalind stared down at the toes of her shoes, unable to look at him—"I'm sorry, but I can't go wi' you."

"I know." The surprise in his voice caused her to look upward. He seemed almost offended. "I wouldn't ask that of you, Rosalind. To separate from family. . . 'Tis a horrible thing."

"Then"—her brow furrowed in confusion—"what decision would you hae me make?" *What else is there for me to decide?*

"Whether I go on wi' the railroad for now or make arrangements to stay the winter."

"Oh!" Rosalind threw her arms around him. "I'm so very glad!" She drew back after her initial burst of excitement and considered. "Won't the railroad need you? I'd not hae you leave them in the lurch when you've made a commitment. That you're a man of your word is one o' the things I admire so "

"Wi' winter coming on, the pace will slow. Johnny's capable of managing on his own by now. He's skilled enough." Ewan's gaze ran deep enough for her to drown in. "'Tis my commitment to you I wouldn't want questioned."

"Oh." Rosalind suddenly found it difficult to speak past the lump in her throat. *If he asked me to go wi' him right this minute, I'd say yes. 'Tis good he will do no such thing!*

"But we've only been courting a wee while. I do not want to put you off by making such a decision wi'out speaking wi' you first." His eyes twinkled with suppressed mirth. "A wonderful lass once warned me against such terrible folly."

"And right she was. 'Tis grateful I am that such a wise woman took pains to show you the error of your ways." She gave him a sidelong smile. " 'Twill make you a much better neighbor this winter." She watched the grin break out across his face and knew she'd not regret her choice.

"I've a sneaking suspicion that same lass will find many ways to make a better man of me." They started back.

"Do you know," Rosalind teased, "I think you might be right."

At the sight of Johnny seated next to Marlene with his arm around her shoulders, Rosalind stopped walking. "Ewan, have you discussed this wi' Johnny to make sure he won't resent it?"

"Aye." He stepped back to stand beside her. Her sudden stop had left him ahead. "Johnny all but insisted I stay behind. Says he needs to have someone he trusts watch o'er Marlene while he's away for the winter. He plans to return come springtime."

" 'Tis good." Rosalind began walking once more but gave a loud sigh. " 'Twould be perfect if Johnny could stay wi' you. I know Marlene will miss him something awful in the months ahead." *And 'twill only be the harder when she sees that I still hae you.* She left the last thought unspoken. She wouldn't say anything that could reflect poorly on her friend. Marlene was entitled to some sadness at the loss of her first true love.

"We'll be sure to include Marlene in fun outings so she won't have time enough to dwell on his absence." Ewan folded her hand in his and gave a reassuring squeeze. "Spring will be upon us before she knows it, and for now, she has you. Such a blessing as that cannot be o'erlooked for very long."

Rosalind gave a gentle squeeze in return but said nothing as they came to stand next to Marlene and Johnny.

Marlene's sobs wracked her petite frame, though Johnny spoke soothing words, promises he would return and they'd be strong for one another. "But I d–don't understand," Marlene gasped. "Why can't you stay if Ewan is going to? Why are you so set on leaving?"

"Now, sugar-pie," Johnny patted her back as one would an upset child's, bungling the earnest attempt to pacify her. "With Ewan gone, they'll need me all the more. We can't both abandon the crew all winter. They've no other blacksmith."

"Why doesn't Ewan go?" Marlene wailed, obviously only realizing the ugliness behind the words after she said them. "I don't mean that I don't want him to stay, too, but why are *you* going on with the railroad while *he* stays here in town?" There was no hiding the tinge of bitter accusation in the question.

Rosalind gaped at her in disbelief. Surely her best friend hadn't spoken such awful words? What would Ewan think?

"Marlene!" Johnny's stern disapproval startled her enough to stop the tears. "Ewan has every bit as much of a right to stay as I do. I counted on you easing his way while I went on ahead. Had someone told me to expect such an objection from my sweet sugar-pie, I wouldn't have believed it."

"I—I didn't mean it that way," Marlene sniffled apologetically. "Really, I do want Rose to be happy."

"That's my Marlene," Johnny encouraged. "Truth be told, Ewan is doing me a great favor by stepping down. I'll no longer be paid as only an apprentice. By sometime this spring, I'll be able to come back to you with enough to start a small home."

"Oh, Johnny," she breathed, "do you mean it?"

"Of course I do!" He apparently couldn't refrain from adding, "It's only what I've been saying this whole time."

"Ewan, Rose, I'm so sorry for what I said." Marlene grasped their entwined hands in hers. "I wouldn't have you leave for my sake, Ewan. Really, truly I wouldn't."

Her earnest tone told Rosalind her best friend had earlier spoken out of frantic desperation. She forgave her on the spot. "I know that." Rosalind disengaged her hand to hug her friend. "This gives us that much more to look forward to come spring." She looked at Ewan and happiness bubbled inside her heart. *Though I hope there are things to look forward to now, as well.*

☙

"Arthur?" Ewan made a beeline for the smithy as soon as he had a chance that afternoon. He waited for the older man's hammer to stop ringing before he went on. "I've a question to ask you."

"I assumed as much." Arthur's smile took the barb from the words. "Though I should warn you that Marlene spilled the news at lunch. I know you've spoken wi' Rosey and decided to stay the winter. I'll not be standing in your way, Ewan."

" 'Tis glad I am to hear it," Ewan said. "Now that I've made the decision, I'll have to find a way to make it work. I was wondering whether you could tell me who used to live in the smaller house so close to your own? As near as I can tell, 'tisn't in use."

"Ah. That used to be Gilda's home. She lived there wi' Cade—they were Kaitlin's parents you ken—up until Cade passed on two years ago." He shrugged. " 'Twasn't safe to let her live alone at her age, and she said the place held too many memories of Cade while she was grieving. So you've the right o' it. Gilda stays wi' us, and the house has stood empty for a bit." He cast Ewan a sidelong glance. "I know Brent Freimont hoped to purchase it as a home not too far in the future."

"Brent Freimont?" Ewan recalled the youth's treatment of Rosalind at the corn husking and his menacing glare after Ewan claimed his kiss. "He'll be having no need of it," he stated flatly. "Do I have your approval?"

"Aye," Arthur agreed. "Rosey has never looked on Brent wi' the affection he bears for her. 'Twouldn't hae been a good match."

"Do I speak wi' you or Gilda about renting the house through winter?" Ewan smiled at Arthur's assessment of Brent.

"I'm all for it, but you'll have to speak wi' Gilda. Though she lives wi' us, 'tis still the home of her heart."

"And I'll treat it as such." He thought of Rosalind's grandmam, the roadmap of wrinkles around her loving gaze and the way she'd locked him over when they first met. "She's a good woman, and I'll not be showing disrespect to her memories. Should she decide not to let me have the place, 'twill be simple enough to build a small soddy." He thought of living half underground, shut in by snow and walled in by solid earth for months at a time. He'd bear with dirt and burrowing bugs to win Rosalind, but all the same... "I do hope Gilda will let me rent the house."

"She'll be at home now, if you're half so anxious to ask as I'm thinking you are." Arthur gave him a wry smile. "Gilda seems to have taken a liking to you, if that helps."

"I'll take all the advantages I can get when it comes t' courting your daughter." Ewan nodded his appreciation and began to leave the smithy. "My thanks for your advice, Arthur."

He set off on the pleasant walk to the MacLean homestead. *Lord, if 'tisn't Your will that I stay in the house, I'll accept that. You know I hope to make Rosalind my bride, but I've yet to see how to do so wi'out either taking her from her family or taking part of her da's livelihood. I can't do either, nor can I ignore the feelings I bear for Rosalind herself. Before winter ends, I pray that You will show me how to proceed. I will not ask her to be my wife until I'm sure 'tis Your will, though I know 'twill be a temptation. Help*

*me remember to seek You first, Father, so I don't lead Rosalind the
wrong way.*

By the time he reached the house, Ewan felt the mantle of
peace that was God's way of showing him he did the right
thing. He raised his fist to knock on the door only to have it
swing open before his hand met the wood even once. Gilda
Banning stood on the other side of the threshold, eyes canny.

"So you've come to ask about the house, hae you?" Her
assessment left him speechless for a moment, and she let out
a gleeful chuckle. "Come in, come in, then. Kaitlin and Luke
went to gather some vegetables from the garden. We'll have a
nice chat, you and I."

"Thank you." Ewan stepped inside, still thrown off balance
by her greeting. "How did you know why I came before I
asked?"

"I've seen a good many years, lad." She sank into a carved
rocker near the hearth. "I know you've come to talk about my
home same as I know Brent Freimont had an eye on it, as
well."

He took a ladder-back chair and dragged it beside her. "I do
not seek it as a wedding gift," Ewan spoke carefully.

"I should hope not!" Gilda snorted. "After knowing our
Rose for less than a month, you know how special she is, but
you'd be a fool t' propose a marriage so very soon."

"Aye," Ewan agreed, relieved that he wouldn't have to defend
himself on that score. "I come to ask whether I might rent
your lovely house for the duration of the winter, and perhaps a
bit into the spring. I'll pay well, Mrs. Banning."

"And 'twill be well worth the price, to my way of thinking."
The old woman rocked slowly, as though contemplating the
matter. "I've not much inside, you see, but I did leave a table

an' chairs and an empty trunk or so. It has a fireplace rather than a stove, but I'd suppose you know that from the size o' the chimney." She nodded and suddenly turned a gimlet eye on him. "What are your intentions toward my granddaughter, Mr. Gailbraith, if you do not ask to buy the place after all?"

"I intend to court her honorably, Mrs. Banning."

"Psh. Call me Gilda." The old woman kept her gaze pinned on him. "And I knew you were honorable, else Arthur wouldn't let you court Rose, and my granddaughter wouldn't see you, and I wouldn't hae allowed you to rent my house." She leaned forward intently. "I mean, what are your plans after you win her, lad? Will you settle here or take her away wi' you?"

"That I cannot say at the moment," Ewan confessed. "I've more than enough money saved t' settle into a home, but Saddleback already has a fine blacksmith in Arthur. Just the same, I don't believe in separating families." He noted the spark of understanding in her eyes. "What answer would you hae wanted?"

"That, I cannot say, lad." She leaned back once more. "We, of course, want her to stay, but that is our desire, not necessarily hers. Our Rose thirsts for a bit o' adventure. She feels she missed her big chance, being just a babe when my Kaitlin brought her to wilds of the Montana Territory. She can't recall the journey, after all, and wants to see a bit o' the world."

"And I'm no closer to an answer." Ewan shifted in the chair. "I appreciate your insight, Gilda, and your generosity."

"As I appreciate yours. Now"—she smiled—"let's talk about the terms of that rental."

eleven

"Marlene didn't take it very well when we packed up the supplies left at the diner." Rosalind frowned. "I wonder how long she'll be so blue. Surely this mood cannot last through the winter!"

"It won't." Mam stirred the hot tallow to keep it from lumping. "But the diner bore memories of her Johnny, and it brought her sadness to the surface. Give her a bit o' time."

"Aye." Grandmam dipped her too-thin candle in the wax again and drew it out, holding it aloft to harden. "She'll come 'round."

"I'm going to make the thickest candle ever." Luke eyed his already too-big contribution. "I'll make it thick enough that when I level the bottom, 'twill stand on its own."

"And if not," Grandmam noted, "we'll melt it down again. 'Twill not be a waste either way, and who knows? It may work."

Rosalind kept her doubts on the matter to herself, instead admiring the soft lavender-blue color of the candles. With each new layer of cooled wax, they took on a slightly darker shade.

" 'Twas so clever to soak the dried blueberries so they plumped and then juice them. It adds such a nice scent and lovely color." She dipped her candle once more and judged it to be thick enough. Rosalind hung it on the drying rack and began again. "The only drawback is they might make us hungry!"

"Mayhap next time we'll add a splash of oil of lilac instead of the blueberry juice." Mam surveyed the filling rack with satisfaction. "We'll be glad to have these come winter."

"Aye," Grandmam seconded. "If there's anything worse than being snowed in for months on end, 'tis being snowed in wi' only the hearth's light to see by. Makes it that much darker."

"Mam, may I give Marlene a candle or two for her nightstand?" Rosalind gave an appreciative sniff. "The treat might help to restore her good spirits. Coax a smile, even."

"I'm sure we can spare a few for such a good cause."

"You can give her mine, Rose." Luke generously held out the large, misshapen candle he'd been nursing the entire day.

"Oh, I'm not sure if 'twill fit in her candleholder, Luke." Rosalind gestured toward the monstrosity. "Best you keep it to read by. 'Twill be interesting to see how long 'twill last."

"Good idea, Rose." Luke headed back to dunk the thing yet again. "I don't think anyone's ever made one like this before."

"I believe you are the first, Luke." Mam ruffled his hair.

"Why don't you run o'er with these four?" Grandmam held them out to Rosalind. "You'll probably be glad to take a nice, quiet walk." Her eyes held a knowing glint as she looked at Rosalind.

"Aye." Rosalind took them thankfully. For the first time since the leaves had turned color, she'd have a moment to herself. With the railroad crew packed off, she could walk alone again.

She draped a light shawl about her shoulders to ward off the chill that warned of winter and set out down the well-worn path. The scents of fallen leaves and rich, dark earth freed by the harvest filled her senses as she moved along.

Father, I see the work of Your hands around me, and 'tis wondrous. Your imagination so far surpasses my own—all I seem to be able to think of is Ewan. How did he go from a man my parents warned me against to my possible future husband in such a short span of time? I remember praying not so long ago about trying to separate out my own impressions of the man wi' the caution Mam and Da exhorted me to use.

Now he has Da's approval, and while Mam had hoped for Brent as a son-in-law, she hasn't spoken against Ewan's courtship. Grandmam has even agreed to rent her house to him for the winter. Everything seems to point to an ideal match—can it be so easy? I know You guard o'er the seasons in our lives, but this time of beginnings seems almost too sweet. Why am I holding a fear that 'twon't last? Help me to trust in Your will, Father, as time ripens.

She knocked on the Freimonts' door, waiting until Mrs. Freimont opened it and ushered her inside with a welcoming smile.

"Rose! It is always good to see you." She took Rosalind's hands in hers and spoke more softly. "Perhaps you can cheer Marlene from her sullens. I will give her the rest of today to adjust to the idea of waiting for her young man, but that is enough."

"Aye." Rosalind nodded. " 'Twouldn't do to stay so for long. I'll hae a chat wi' her. She'll pull through this difficulty."

"Ja." Mrs. Freimont waved for her to go up into the loft where Marlene's bed reposed. Rosalind guessed that her friend had been up there since they'd come back from the diner.

"Marlene!" she called out in a hearty voice as she ascended the ladder. "I've come to see how you're doing this afternoon." She poked her head over the ladder to find Marlene sitting atop her bed, evidence of recent tears staining her white pillowcase.

Not a good sign, Rosalind inventoried, *though she's not crying* now. That's more hopeful. Oh, unless she's cried so much she can't cry anymore. And I thought some blue candles would help?

"Don't stand on the ladder all day," Marlene sniffed. "Come on up." She patted the mattress beside her and gave a ghost of a smile. "I promise I won't say anything awful."

"Hush." Rosalind stooped into the loft and sat beside Marlene. "I brought you a little something." She passed over the candles.

"They're purple! No, blue?" Marlene squinted in an attempt to determine. "Whatever did you put in the wax for color?"

"Mam added blueberry juice, and I thought they were a little more blue than purple, though I wouldn't argue wi' you on the matter." Rosalind took a deep breath. "Smell them."

"Mmm. . ." Marlene inhaled a few times before she put the candles down. "They make me want to eat some blueberries."

" 'Tis almost the same thing as what I said!" Rosalind laughed. "Still, I think 'twas a marvelous idea. Think of all the different things we could use! Raspberries for summer, apples for fall—and the berries at least would turn the whole batch pink."

"Custom candles," Marlene said. "Think of it—candles to match the color of your quilt or curtains, whichever you like."

"What would you use for green or yellow?" Rosalind tried to think of anything that would work. "I can only think of green beans or such, and I wouldn't want that scent all the time."

"Nor I." Marlene thought a moment. "We could stir pumpkin juice with a stick of cinnamon and see how that turns out."

"Maybe. That would give us something like yellow. But I don't like the smell of raw pumpkin o'ermuch—just baked."

"That's what the cinnamon is for, Rose." Marlene leaned back on her elbows and stared up at the ceiling rafters. "I can't believe he's already gone. Here yesterday, and today—"

"Working to save up for your wedding," Rosalind broke in. "And we both know your da would say you're too young to wed for a while yet. Johnny's doing what's best for your future, Marlene. He'll come back."

"Do you really think so?" Marlene plucked at a loose string on her quilt. "He won't meet some other girl before then?"

"Not one who could cast you from his memory. God made you special, and none can compare." Rosalind's heart ached at her friend's forlorn look. "He'll be back afore you know it."

"I'll know it the second my Johnny walks back into town," Marlene declared with her old confidence. "I know it will take a year or two before our home is ready—it takes so long to clear land, raise a house, and start a farm—but at least he'll be with me then. For now, I'll just have to think about something else." She looked at Rosalind with a speculative gaze. "So, how do you plan to get Ewan to propose?"

twelve

"No, not like that." Grandmam shooed Rosalind away from the stuffed goose. "You keep it in the juices so it stays moist."

"I'd thought to add flour and such to make a bit o' gravy." Rosalind shrugged and slid a loaf of pumpkin spice bread from the old niche at the hearth. When Mam and Da first built the house, they'd not had a stove to call their own. Now, for Thanksgiving Day, every cooking contraption had been called into service.

"You make it right," Mam sided against Rosalind, "and there's no need for gravy."

"Da likes it for his potatoes and dressing," Rosalind pointed out. " 'Tis no insult to the bird."

"Aye." Grandmam's shoulders relaxed. "My Cade loved a dribble of thick gravy on his mashed potatoes, too. But you wait until the last possible moment—not until after the Thanksgiving Meeting."

"Right." Rosalind pinned an errant curl behind her ear. "I should hae remembered that. When did I become such a muddled miss?"

"Oh"—Mam gave her a sideways look—"I'd say about the same time Ewan decided to stay through the lonely winter."

"Mam!" Rosalind shook her head but smiled at the truth in her mother's words. " 'Tis happy I am we've so much to be thankful for this Thanksgiving Day."

"And you want it to come off just right"—Grandmam

shuffled back to her rocker—"and make sure you show Ewan he's made a sound decision, that's what 'tis."

"I hope I'm never so ungrateful as to o'erlook the others I'm blessed with." Rosalind walked over to give the old woman a hug. "Ewan's not the only one I thank God for."

"Aye." Mam came by to join the embrace. "Rose has the right o' it."

"All the same"—Grandmam settled back more comfortably after the moment passed—"I've the notion you ought to wear your best blue dress for the festivities today, Rose. It draws attention to your sparkling eyes."

"I'd already planned to," she admitted. "After all, Thanksgiving is a time when we thank the Lord by putting forth our best efforts!"

"Aye." Da stepped into the warmth of the house, trailed by Luke. " 'Tis glad I am to hear my women speak such humble thoughts."

Rosalind raised her eyebrows toward Mam and Grandmam—they had, after all, just been discussing a sort of vanity. Neither gave the slightest hint of amusement but carried on as though Da had the right of it.

It brought to mind Grandmam's old lesson: A still tongue gathers praise when a busy one catches naught but air.

"Luke!" Rosalind gently slapped his hand away from one of the carefully arranged platters of food. "You know that's for the community dinner!"

"But picnic eggs are my favorite!" His brown eyes pled for a wee taste.

"Just one." Rosalind handed him one of the boiled eggs, hollowed and refilled with a mashed mix of yolk, lard, pickle brine, and salt. They happened to be a favorite of hers, too.

She popped one into her own mouth as she rearranged the platter to cover the empty spaces they'd made.

"We'll change into our Sunday best and make our way to the Freimonts' for the special Thanksgiving service." Da's declaration was the cue for everyone to fly into action, readying themselves to leave.

Rosalind helped prepare the dishes she, Mam, and Grandmam had worked on since the day before for carrying to Delana's kitchen. This Thanksgiving would bring a feast the likes of which Saddleback had never seen before!

With the work done, Rosalind slipped into her blue cotton dress, straightening the crisp white collar that framed her face with starched purity. She smoothed her hair one last time and pulled on her cloak and gloves.

"Is everyone ready?" Da turned to check, and Ma plunked the platter bearing the stuffed goose into his open arms.

Everyone else took up a dish or two before stepping outside, and Rosalind found Ewan about to knock on their door. She favored him with a smile as he took the basket of biscuits from her and offered her his arm.

"Thank you." She slipped her hand into the warm crook of his elbow and set off.

"My pleasure." He took care to shorten his stride, going slowly so she wouldn't have to rush to keep alongside him.

Such a thoughtful man. She peeked up at him. *And such a handsome one.* The Lord had outdone Himself the day He fashioned Ewan Gailbraith, and she meant to give thanks for it. After all, it wasn't every day a girl walked before the town in her best dress, on the arm of a kind, handsome suitor as they prepared to praise God for another wonderful year. No, days just didn't get any better than this.

The wide Montana sky stretched before them, clear as could be. The air crisped with the nip of winter's cold, but the sunshine chased thoughts of snow away. They reached the Freimonts' home in a few moments—far too soon, to Rosalind's way of thinking. She reluctantly slipped her hand from Ewan's arm, taking back the biscuits and following the women into Delana's kitchen.

The warm fragrance of baked apples wrapped itself around her like a welcome as she set the basket on one of two already-too-full tables. Pies, loaves of flavored breads, biscuits, muffins, corn cake, and maple sweeties vied for space between roasted chicken, turkey, and goose. Dishes of mashed potatoes, sweet potatoes, dressing, coleslaw, and Rosalind's deviled eggs crowded in alongside. She'd never seen such a feast—the women of the town had really outdone themselves this year. But though the kitchen seemed full of busy women, several of them were missing.

Rosalind took a swift tally. Jakob and Isaac Albright's mail-order brides bustled back and forth importantly as Delana and Marlene worked furiously over the red-hot stove. Mam, having made sure all the dishes were deposited in the warmth of the kitchen, was bundling Grandmam into a chair in the corner. A glance out the window showed the Twadley girls, along with the Hornton and Preston women, hovering close by, fingering each others' woolen capes and laughing in the spirit of the day. The men plunked benches into neat rows, preparing for the Thanksgiving service.

Rosalind gave a deep sigh of satisfaction. *All present and accounted for.* By God's grace, everyone in the entire community had gathered to give thanks.

Rosalind's gaze drifted past the chatting women to where

Ewan held a serious conversation with the Freimont men. The earnestness of his gaze grabbed her heart, and his sudden smile brought a matching one to her own face.

This Thanksgiving, no one has more to be grateful for than I do. Thank You, Jesus, for bringing Ewan into my life. 'Tis more than I'd dared hope for.

෴

Ewan looked up from his discussion with Dustin Freimont and spied Rosalind peeking at him through the window. At his quick wave, she grinned and ducked out of sight.

Ah, Lord, thank You for my precious Rosalind. Has it really only been a matter of mere weeks since You brought her into my life? He paused for a moment, considering the fact that he'd arrived in her hometown. *Or rather, You led me to her? Either way, the result is the same—we're together. For that, I'll be forever grateful, Father. Though the winter ahead may seem long and at times lonely when we're snowed in, apart from one another, the knowledge that she's nearby and safe will be a treasure I cherish. The only thing that could make this day—nay, this entire season—better would be if Johnny were here to share his joy wi' Marlene as I am able to share my happiness wi' my Rosalind. Father, keep an eye on the lad as he works through this winter. I've the notion You'll see him work harder than ever before. You've given him a new motivation in little Marlene. Thank You, Father.*

At that final word, a cloud passed over Ewan's bright day, and he frowned in sudden sorrow. *And Lord, please watch o'er my own da, wherever he may be this day.*

Ewan looked up to see the townspeople taking their seats upon the rough benches that served as pews. He scanned the crowd to find Rosalind's family before wending his way toward them and settling himself beside her. As the light fragrance of rosewater reached his senses, he smiled once more.

Dustin Freimont stood before the congregation in lieu of the circuit riding preacher. The man cleared his throat, a last minute call for the attention of those still shifting about. When all were watching, he spoke. "We all know that today is the day of Thanksgiving, where we show our gratitude to the Lord above for the blessings He's given us, and we remind our loved ones how we appreciate them." He stopped to shoot a glance at the pretty, older blond woman Ewan recalled as Dustin's wife, Delana. "I'd like to start the day with a hymn. I believe we all know 'For the Beauty of the Earth.'"

Ewan sat back and let the song wash over him, joining in as the half-forgotten melody grew full with the voices of many.

"For the beauty of the earth,
  for the glory of the skies,
for the love which from our birth
  over and around us lies;
Lord of all, to Thee we raise
  this our hymn of grateful praise."

How fitting, Lord. Wi' the beauty of the glorious skies above us and the rich earth beneath our feet, we are truly surrounded by Your love.

"For the joy of human love,
  brother, sister, parent, child;
friends on earth and friends above;
  for all gentle thoughts and mild:

Lord of all, to Thee we raise
this our hymn of grateful praise."

*And this. When for the first time in years I am wi' people I
love as I would family. And wi' Rosalind, who I bear husbandly
affection for although we are not yet wed. This is fitting, for 'tis the
people of Saddleback who are its greatest lure, and their souls Your
greatest treasure.*

The hymn came to an end all too quickly, but Ewan listened
closely as Dustin began to speak once again, his Bible open to
the passage he and Ewan had been discussing scant moments
before. "Ewan Gailbraith, a newcomer to Saddleback, saw me
rifling through the pages of my Bible in search of Psalm 65
this morning. And, while it is a wonderful passage advocating
that we thank the Lord for His bounty, I seem to recall
reading the same chapter and verse last year. But the Word of
Christ"—he held up the Bible—"is full of wisdom, and Mr.
Gailbraith directed my attention to the book of Deuteronomy.
I'll be reading from chapter 8 this morning." With a nod to
Ewan, he took a breath as though to begin. But no words came
for a moment.

"Actually"—Mr. Freimont pinned him with an intense
gaze before continuing—"I, for one, would be glad to have
you do the honors."

Ewan blinked as the other man gestured for him to come
up. Several others were nodding, and Rosalind went so far
as to give him an encouraging nudge. He got to his feet and
made his way before the congregation before accepting Mr.
Freimont's Bible.

"This is irregular," Dustin Freimont admitted. "But it seems
to me that the verse is fitting, and it's equally fitting to have

the man who chose it be the one to speak on it." With this, he went to sit beside his wife, leaving Ewan alone before the population of Saddleback.

"Well,"—Ewan cleared his throat—"I can't say I've ever filled in for a preacher before, so I apologize in advance for my inexperience. That being said, this is a verse I keep dear to my heart, and I hope you'll do the same.

"Deuteronomy, chapter 8, verses 7 through 10: 'For the Lord thy God bringeth thee into a good land, a land of brooks of water, of fountains and depths that spring out of valleys and hills; a land of wheat, and barley, and vines, and fig trees, and pomegranates; a land of oil olive, and honey; a land wherein thou shalt eat bread without scarceness, thou shalt not lack any thing in it; a land whose stones are iron, and out of whose hills thou mayest dig brass. When thou hast eaten and art full, then thou shalt bless the Lord thy God for the good land which he hath given thee.'"

Ewan paused to let the words sink in. "Now, I hadn't thought to speak on this passage, but a few things do come to my mind. First is that the Lord our God has brought us all into a good land, a land of brooks of water, valleys and hills, and wheat. . . . Those words weren't written about the Montana Territory, but they certainly do an excellent job of describing nature's bounty in this area." Several people were nodding, and he warmed to his speech.

"And when I see the good folk who've settled here, sensing that God has been welcomed into this community—and smell the food in the kitchen—it seems to me that we don't lack any good thing. And how appropriate 'tis that verse 10 speaks of eating and being physically full of the things God has given us in His care for our souls, that we may bless Him for all He's given us." He looked around, giving just one more comment. "So it seems to me, we should get to that eating so we can bless Him with full hearts and bellies!"

The men chortled their approval and everyone clapped, nodding their agreement with Ewan's assessment.

"Before we sit down to enjoy the fruits of our labors and the skills of our women's hands, I'd like to lead us in a simple praise—an old favorite." Ewan tilted back his head and sang the verse, singing it again as the townspeople joined in:

> "Praise God from whom all blessings flow;
>   praise Him, all creatures here below;
> Praise Him above, ye heavenly host;
>   praise Father, Son and Holy Ghost. Amen."

As they all sat down to the best spread Ewan had ever seen in his life, he looked over at Rosalind, and the words of praise echoed in his mind once again.

Your blessings hae flowed upon me, Jesus. I praise You above all others, and thank You for Your loving grace. Amen.

thirteen

After being uninhabited for so long, this place needs a bit o' upkeep, Ewan mused after a night spent trying to bundle up against chill drafts. *I'll see if I can get some pitch to fill in those gaps.*

He gulped his too-hot coffee in an attempt to warm up and ate his fried eggs straight from the pan. *No sense making extra dishes to wash when no one's around to quibble about niceties.*

Then he went to the firmly shut curtains and thrust them aside, eager to see the glow of the sun—and the warmth it promised. After working a forge for so many years, heat was more natural to him than cold would ever be.

He blinked at the view before him. *Snow!* A blanket of white covered the ground, coated tree branches, and dusted his windowpane. *No wonder 'twas so cold—a snowstorm blew in o'ernight.* Ewan pulled on an extra pair of socks, then struggled to jam his boots over them. He took his coat from the peg by the door and slid it over his shoulders before plunking on his seldom-used hat and mittens. Blacksmiths rarely had use for the things.

Girding himself for a cold wind, he opened the door and stepped outside. Before he so much as drew a breath of fresh air, something whizzed over to plunk on his jacket.

"I got him!" Luke pointed at him. "Did you see that throw? I just aimed and *thwunk*, he didn't know until 'twas too late!"

While the lad all but danced with pride, Ewan crouched

down and scooped up some snow of his own. Packing it into a round ball, he waited for the right moment before he let it fly. *Whooosh-umph*, his snowball soared toward the boy, only to be intercepted by another expertly thrown one. He scowled as both burst into harmless pieces and fell softly to the ground. Then he looked to see who'd interfered with the lad's just desserts.

"Rosalind?" He looked in disbelief to where his lass, bundled in a woolen cloak, calmly packed her next volley. "You're firing at me?" Ewan put the shock of betrayal in his tone.

"Now, Ewan, I did no such thing." She neatly placed yet another snowball in the line before her. "I fired at your snowball. That's an entirely different matter, you know." The laughter in her voice made it hard not to smile in return.

"Two against one is clear as day," he growled. "This means war." He began packing snow as quickly as he could scoop it up, his jacket bearing the wet stains attesting to his opponents' ruthlessness. "Who fires on an unarmed man?" he roared, letting fly a few of his own shots. "Take that, and that, and—mmph!" A snowball hit him smack in the mouth before he'd truly begun.

"Nice one, Rose!" Luke shrieked with merriment, laughing so hard he began to cough.

"That's enough, now," Rosalind kicked apart her snowballs in a show of truce before walking over to her brother. "Let's go in for a sip o' cider, shall we?" She tugged his hat down.

"Will you cry craven the moment your opponent is ready to do battle?" Ewan protested the abrupt ending. "Stand and fight, or"—he lobbed a set of snowballs, each finding one of the siblings across the way—"surrender!"

"I said that's enough." The tightness in Rosalind's tone took him by surprise. "If you want some cider, come inside wi' us.' She shooed young Luke into the warmth of the house and marched in behind him, leaving Ewan standing alone.

What? I've never thought o' Rosalind as fickle, but she abandoned the challenge quickly enough. Something hae set her back up, and 'tis best I find out what afore I make another misstep. Surely a reason lies behind her change of heart.

He resolutely made his way to the still-open door of the house. *There's a good sign, at least.* Ewan stomped the snow from his boots before venturing into the MacLean home.

Arthur raised a hand in greeting, Mrs. MacLean poured cider into mugs, and Luke, seated beside the roaring fire, coughed after sending some of his drink down the wrong way. Ewan noticed that Rosalind hadn't taken off her warm cloak.

"Ewan, would you walk me to the barn?" She laid a small, gloved hand on his arm. "I've yet to check on the livestock."

"O' course." Ewan led her out the door, walking with her in silence on the short trek to the barn. He waited.

"I wanted to apologize for being so curt." She stood before him, her hands worrying the fabric of her skirts. " 'Twas rude and uncalled for. 'Twill not happen again, Ewan, I promise."

"I thought that last snowball must have hit harder than I intended. Don't worry that I took offense at it, Rosalind."

"Aye. But in the future"—she looked up at him, big blue eyes earnest and pleading—"when I say 'tis time to go inside, I will ask that you not question it. The cold weather makes it all too easy to catch chill, and we've no doctor hereabouts."

" 'Tis wise of you to take care, Rosalind. I hadn't thought of the lack of doctors out here, and the last thing I would want is for you to catch ill." He could scarcely stand to speak of the possibility. "As soon as you say the word, I'll take you back inside. You've my word on it, and that's all you need."

"Thank you." She looked as though she wanted to say more but paused before adding, "Trust is a foundation to build on."

"Aye, Rosalind." He covered her shoulder with his hand. "And I'm aiming to build something to last a lifetime."

❧

"Hae we enough snow to build a man?" Luke peered through the frost-covered window after the second snowstorm days later.

"There will be," Rosalind judged. "For now, we wait for the storm to end and the sun to come out and soften it for us." *And warm the frigid air enough so you can play awhile wi'out gasping for breath and coughing. Even then, 'twill be a small snowman. All too soon you'll be spending your days and nights near the warmth of the fire. Best to enjoy the outdoors for now.*

"This time I want to make a great big one." Luke stretched a hand above his head. "With Ewan to help, we can do it this year. Last time 'twas a sad and puny man we made, to be sure."

"Last year's snowman was my favorite," Grandmam spoke up as she rocked back and forth. "Reminded me of you when you were that small. 'Twould be better to build two of those than one great big man. Everyone tries t' build the same old thing."

"Oh." Luke frowned as he thought it over. "Maybe we'll try to make a small one and a big one, so they're friends."

"As long as the small one comes first, for Grandmam." Rosalind gave her a conspiratorial smile. They both knew Luke would only be able to make a small one, and should he start after his larger goal, would protest leaving it unfinished.

"Aye," Luke agreed generously, "for our grandmam." He hopped up and went over to press a kiss on her wrinkled cheek.

Rosalind smiled and continued knitting the scarf she planned for Ewan. *He doesn't hae one, and though he says nothing, I see that the cold bothers him just as it does Da. Fire is their element, and ice doesna agree wi' blacksmiths.*

In my worry o'er Luke, I was harsh wi' Ewan. He doesn't know of Luke's weakness, though he'll find out afore too long. For now, Luke lights up at the way Ewan treats him—like any regular lad. So long as it poses no risk, we'll let it be.

Her fingers stiff, Rosalind put away her knitting and went over to the trunk where the family Bible was kept. Kneeling, she drew it out, feeling cracks in the worn leather cover. She opened it to the first pages, full of family records.

Tears pricked her eyes at the names of Cade Banning and James MacLean. Her grandda and her baby brother were the most recent in a chain of loss stretching back over decades. She ran her fingers over the ink.

Gone but not forgotten. How long will it be until Grandmam's name joins that of her husband's? And how many harsh winters will Luke weather? Ten? Twenty? Will he marry and have wee ones of his own? I pray 'tis so.

Her gaze came to rest on the marriage register. It was Da's Bible, and so did not bear the date of Rosalind's grandparents' wedding. She traced the names of her parents—Arthur MacLean and Kaitlin Banning. *Will mine and Ewan be the next names written and kept here for our children to read someday?*

She turned the fine, brittle pages to the chapter she sought—

Ecclesiastes 3—and read to herself. *"To every thing there is a season, and a time to every purpose under the heaven: A time to be born, and a time to die; a time to plant, and a time to pluck up that which is planted."*

Life and death, side by side in the family records, and placed together in scripture, as well. Joy tempered with sorrow; a balance struck between the two.

Lord, all things are to come in Your time. As the seasons change, so, too, do we. This winter seems the most important season I've ever faced. Please help me grow into the woman You'd hae me be and, if 'tis Your plan, the woman Ewan will love. Come spring, a new beginning will bloom all around—I'll say honestly that I hope for a piece of that wellspring in my own life.

Rosalind carefully closed the Bible and placed it in the trunk once more. She looked up to see Da watching her, a question in his gaze. Ma unfolded extra quilts to place on the beds—the hearth wouldn't stave off cold when darkness fell.

I've not seen Ewan in two days. Only two days into a storm, and it seems as though he's been gone from me for weeks. He's snowed in, same as we are. Only Da goes outside, using the guideline to the barn.

Grandmam's house—and Ewan—sat much too far away to string a guideline. It was part of the reason she'd moved. With no way of knowing when the storm would end, Rosalind couldn't even look forward to a day she'd see him again. Marlene endured a distance much greater but with certain knowledge to help her bide her time.

It seems almost a worse torture to know Ewan is so close, but that I can't reach him. Rosalind took up her knitting once more. *Does he regret the decision we made? Is he wishing he had gone* on wi' the railroad—wi' Johnny for companionship and work to hasten the long hours? My Ewan works hard day in and day out—how can he stand being cooped up in four walls, all alone, wi' so little to keep him occupied?

Rosalind looked to the blocked window and couldn't help but wonder, *Is he thinking of me while I think of him?*

fourteen

Ewan shoved back the curtain without much hope of seeing anything but the wall of white that had stood between him and Rosalind for days on end. Was it wishful thinking or could he see the faint yellow glow of sunlight through the thinning snow?

Yes. . .yes. The blizzard has passed, and the sun is beginning its work. Soon I'll see my Rosalind again.

Ewan stoked the fire and put on some coffee before starting the porridge.

Lord, 'tis by Your grace I had the time to prepare for the winter ahead. Weeks ago, I'd worried 'twas too soon to ask Rosalind whether I should stay through the winter. Now I see 'twas Your timing, ensuring I could chop enough wood to last the cold of the winter.

I'd wondered whether 'twould drive me half mad, being trapped within four walls wi' no work to do and no one wi' whom to speak or pass the time. I was wrong to doubt the wisdom of Your will.

For too long I've worked, focusing on what needed to be done, falling onto my pallet at night wi' only the time to thank You for seeing me through the day and giving me a livelihood. I traveled across this new world, at first in search of my father, then in search of solace from my failure. Yet in all that searching, I lost my true focus.

Now I've taken time to seek You as I hae not in too many years. I don't deserve the grace of Your love nor the joy I find in Rosalind, but I treasure both. In the barren sleep of winter, a new beginning stirs to life. I aim to not lose sight of that, Lord.

Whistling, Ewan added a pinch of brown sugar to his porridge. He poured a mug full of the strong, steaming coffee, leaving it black. When he pushed away from the table, his glance fell on the just-finished project in the corner.

"More evidence of Your timing, Lord. Those snowshoes will come in handy soon," Ewan determined aloud. He opened the door of the house to a blockage of thick snow, scooped some into the pot he'd used to make the oatmeal, and cleaned it. He filled it with icy white once more before shutting the door and returning to the hearth.

While the water heated, Ewan dug out his razor and strop. With sharpened blade, small mirror, and warmed water, he set to. The raspy *scrape* of the razor, punctuated by an occasional *swish* in the water, filled the still house. Ewan ran a hand over his now-smooth jaw and nodded at his reflection. *Now I'm ready to see Rosalind.*

The strong, bitter scent of his coffee had him reaching for the mug again. He drained it in one long swallow. He looked around the cabin, checking off items. *Morning devotions done, bed made, breakfast eaten, pot cleaned, face shaven, snowshoes finished.*

He drummed his fingers on the tabletop. *I wonder. . .* He peered through the curtains again. *Maybe.* He grabbed the poker from the hearth and swung the door open again, giving the wall of ice an experimental prod. Since the door wasn't on the same side of the house as the window, the wall of snow here might be thicker. *Hmm.* No snow rumbled forward to fill the gap. He cautiously worked the poker farther and farther until his arm was thrust into the snow at the top of the door.

Finally, there was no resistance. The snow, already thawing, piled only a few feet outside the door!

Ewan withdrew and shut the door, warming his half-frozen arm by the fire before donning his jacket, hat, and worn mittens. With the aid of the poker, he broke a sizeable opening through the snowbank and watched as the top portion collapsed down. Ewan kicked through it, smiling at the sight of the snowy hill nearby that must be Rosalind's home.

With the fire banked and his snowshoes tightly strapped to his boots, Ewan made his way. It was slow going, putting one foot before the other, cautiously testing the firm pack of snow before transferring his weight. Finally, he stood before the mound, seeing a corner of the roof poking out of the snowy whiteness.

Will it seem odd that I didn't wait a wee while longer for the snow to clear on its lonesome? Ewan's gloved hands clenched. *No matter. Everyone will be as eager as I am to taste some fresh air.* He dug into the snow, pushing it aside until he reached the wall. *It fell more deeply here—'tis far thicker.* Ewan tapped on the unearthed windowpane, waited, and tapped again before the curtains drew back.

Luke pressed his nose to the windowpane and squinted through the frost. Ewan rubbed the pane clear of ice as Luke disappeared.

Rosalind's eyes widened when she saw him, and Ewan grinned. She pressed one small, bare hand against the glass, and he swiftly pressed his thickly gloved one over it on his side.

"I'll hae you out in a minute!" he yelled, knowing she understood him when she nodded and drew her hand back. He pushed the snow aside feverishly, packing it down in front of the door before giving a mighty knock.

"Ewan!" Rosalind swung the door open, the heated blast of air from within matching the warmth of her gaze. "You're soaking!" She pulled him inside.

❧

Rosalind curled her fingers into the sopping fabric of his coat sleeve, pulling him close.

" 'Twould hae melted soon enough," she chided, tugging the coat from his broad shoulders. She laid it out by the fire and held out her hand for his dripping gloves. She twisted them as dry as she could before turning back. Rosalind found his green eyes watching her with a love that brought a warmth to her heart. He'd not said a word, just let her cluck over him like a fussy hen.

He raised a brow and held out one large hand in a silent invitation. She put her hand in his and stood close, reaching up to cup his clean-shaven cheek. *He shaved for me, just as he broke through the snow for me.*

"I couldn't wait another day." Ewan's deep rumble washed over her as he smoothed his free hand over her hair, his fingertips playing with the end of her braid.

"I'm glad you didn't." She returned his gaze until something new—chagrin?—flickered on his face. For the first time since she'd seen him at the window, Rosalind realized her entire family, from Grandmam all the way down to young Luke, was watching. She glanced at Da. She drew back the hand that cupped Ewan's strong jaw, missing the contact immediately.

"Don't just stand there." Grandmam shook her head, but all could see the smile on her face. "Sit down so Luke can help you with those snowshoes."

"I'll warm some mulled cider." Mam busied herself at the

hearth as everyone sprang into motion.

"Good to see you, Ewan." Da spoke solemnly, but Rosalind heard the humor behind it. He put out his pipe.

"Ewan?" Luke flopped down at his feet, untying the snowshoes. "Will you help me make a snowman? A grand big one?" He held his hand high over his head.

Rosalind cleared her throat.

"Oh." Luke seemed properly chastened. "Two, then. A bitty one for Grandmam first, and then the grand big one?" His voice rose with anxious hope.

"Luke!" Rosalind intervened. "Ewan broke through the snow o'er his place and ours and only just sat before the fire!"

"Indeed," Mam added. "His things are wet with melted ice."

"I know." Luke seemed to shrink into himself, his thin voice tugging at Rosalind's heart. "I thought that so long as he was already snowy, 'twould be a good time, you see." He stacked the snowshoes carefully by the hearth. " 'Twasn't my intent to be rude."

"Nor were you, lad." Ewan's smile robbed the room of any chill of discomfort. "Sound planning, to my way o' thinking. Now, if you can convince your bonny sister to lend a hand, I'd say this is as good a time as any." He shot Rosalind a quick wink.

"Rose?" Luke's shining eyes pled for her assent, and she couldn't withhold it.

"Aye, then. Let's both pile on our winter clothes." Rosalind frowned at Ewan's sodden coat and gloves.

"I've an old coat o' your da's in a trunk hereabouts." Mam moved some embroidered pillowcases off the top of the chest. "Should do a sight better than that mess. Ah, there." She shook out the old garment. "We don't want you catching a chill, Mr. Gailbraith."

"Thank you, Mrs. MacLean." Ewan accepted the coat and turned to Grandmam. "Now, Mrs. Banning, what's all this about a tiny snowman?"

"I'm of the opinion that snowmen should come in different sizes"—Grandmam eyed Ewan as he held Rosalind's winter cloak for her—"just as folks do. The small ones are most often more loveable."

"Aye." Ewan put his hands on Rosalind's shoulders, emphasizing the disparity between their heights. " 'Tis right you are."

"I disagree." Rosalind turned, tilting her head back to look up at him. "Da is a big bear o' a man—same as you."

"And a more loveable fellow I've yet to meet." Mam walked over to Da and smiled up at him.

"Ready!" Luke's proclamation broke the tender moment as he led Rosalind and Ewan outdoors.

"Ooh." The chill wind made Rosalind shiver before she joined her brother. Together, they packed a base for the smaller snowman while Ewan began work on the larger.

Da and Mam came out to join them. "We thought we'd lend a hand."

"Ah." Mam took a deep breath of the clean, crisp air. "So nice to be outside again. And we have you to thank for that, Mr. Gailbraith."

"What use is the wide open when you've no one to share it wi'?" Ewan's smile sent a thrill through Rosalind.

"We're more than happy to share this beautiful day wi' you." Rosalind tried to imbue the words with the depth of her joy but feared she fell far short.

"I think this is done." Luke frowned in concentration as he gauged the base for the tiny snowman. "She wants it small."

"Here." Da plunked a large handful of hardened snow atop Luke's finished portion. "Let's start on the middle."

"I'll go see what branches and such I can find." Mam headed for a copse of trees, leaving Rosalind standing alone.

Since Da helped Luke, she began packing snow to help Ewan. She tacked it onto the already massive chunk he worked to make round.

"How's that?" He stepped back to examine the misshapen lump.

"Well. . ." Rosalind gave the matter due consideration as she stepped around the beginnings of the sculpture. This one level reached her hip! "Seems to me. . ." She crouched down and made a show of inspecting it. "Yes. . .I know what will set it right."

"What?"

"If you look here"—Rosalind gestured him closer and bit back her grin as Ewan moved toward her—"it needs. . ."

"It needs what?" He looked down at the huge snow lump, then back up at her.

"Leveling off," she told him solemnly before shoving a goodly amount of the excess all over him.

"Hey!" Ewan straightened up, brushing snow from his face and shaking it from his coat.

Rosalind laughed as he gave a little dance to free his collar of the icy deluge. He stopped moving. Her breath caught. Bits of the ice clung to Ewan's coal-black hair, catching the winter sunshine as it melted. Standing tall and proud, he was magnificent.

"Rosalind." His voice lingered over her name as though relishing every syllable.

"Oh!" She spluttered as he took advantage of her gawking to

exact revenge. He threw a spray of snow so it coated her. The icy specks melted on her tongue, stung her nose, and trickled into her hair where her cloak fell back. "You'll pay for that, Ewan Gailbraith!" She packed a snowball and advanced on him.

"I hope so." He snagged the snow from her hand and slipped a strong arm around her waist before she could react. His grin had a devilish charm. "I hope I get exactly what I deserve." The warmth in his gaze left no doubt what he meant.

Rosalind opened her mouth to tell him she felt the same. . . then shrieked as she felt her own snowball trickling down her back.

fifteen

"The pond is frozen over!" Luke barreled into the house a week later, his breath coming in hard gasps of excitement.

Ewan slapped his knee. "Well then. Sounds like we're going ice skating." He stood up. "I'll go get my skates and be right back."

"We'll be ready," Rosalind promised. "Though I'd like to go fetch Marlene, if you don't mind."

"You get your friend, I'll get my skates, and you"—Ewan mussed Luke's hair—"get ready." He set out, his long stride quickly covering the distance between the MacLean household and Gilda's house. He opened the trunk where he'd stowed most of his own possessions and withdrew the metal skates.

Holding them by the laces, Ewan walked back to Rosalind's home. Luke met him at the door, flushed and eager.

"Rose isn't back yet." The boy's voice lowered to a confiding whisper. "Marlene always takes a long time to do anything."

Ewan crouched down to look at the lad eye to eye. "Someday you'll see that pretty girls are worth the wait."

"But. . ." Luke frowned. "Rose doesn't make anybody wait if she can help it."

"I know." Ewan gave the lad a wink. "That makes her worth even more." He straightened up and saw the girls approaching . . with a man escorting Rosalind—Brent Freimont.

"Luke," he stooped once more and spoke with urgency, "who is that young man walking wi' your sister?"

"Oh. That's Brent Freimont, Marlene's brother."

"Yes, I know his name." Ewan tried again. "Has he been courting Rosalind for long?"

"Courting? He makes big eyes at her and sits next to her whenever he can." Luke scoffed. "Brent burnt down the outhouse a few months ago."

"He burnt—" Ewan stopped himself. There was more important information he needed right away. "And your sister?"

"No." Luke gave him a strange look. "He didn't burn Rose. 'Twas an accident wi' the privy."

"I meant," Ewan clarified, torn between exasperation and amusement, "did Rose encourage his attentions?" *The lad made a nuisance o' himself at the husking bee, but from the way Rose dismissed him, I thought he was no serious rival.*

"Hardly." Luke snorted. "Everyone hereabouts thought she'd marry Brent, but she looks on him as a brother, same as me. Almost." He thought for a moment. "She likes me better."

"As do I." Ewan patted the boy on the shoulder and stood to his full height as the three companions joined them. His jaw tightened as he saw Brent's hand laid possessively over Rosalind's, which lay nestled in the crook of his arm.

"Thank you, Brent." Rosalind looked anything but pleased as she tried to disentangle.

Ewan's sudden good cheer vanished as Brent tightened his grasp, saying, "Of course, Rose. I'll escort you all the way to the pond. We wouldn't want you to stumble again."

"As I've already told you, Brent, 'twas naught but a bit of snow I was shaking from the top of my boot." Rosalind tugged free at last. "I did not stumble at all." She gave Ewan a beseeching glance.

As Brent reached for her hand once more, Ewan stepped between them. "I'd be pleased to carry your skates, Rosalind."

"Thank you." The heartfelt appreciation in her tone spurred Brent into action.

"I'll do that." He yanked the laces from her hand.

The lad fell for it! "Well, since your hands are full, I'll be happy to escort the lady." Ewan smoothly offered Rosalind his arm. "Miss Freimont"—he gave a slight bow to Marlene—"good to see you."

"And you, Mr. Gailbraith." The amusement in her smile let him know she hadn't missed how he stressed the last word. "You've met my brother, Brent Freimont, haven't you?"

"Oh, we've met." Ewan looked at the lad in disgust before smiling at his sister. "Shall we go on to the pond?"

With that, he and Rosalind led the way, leaving Brent to trail behind. Ewan set a quick pace, deliberately putting more distance between Rosalind and him and the others.

"He needs time to come to terms wi' it, that's all." Rosalind spoke only when they were out of earshot. "Brent has nurtured certain. . .hopes, for a long while now."

"Hopes?" Ewan raised a brow. "Or expectations, Rosalind?"

"Expectations." Her whisper made him uneasy. "Expectations encouraged by his parents and my mother—but not by me." Her blue eyes transfixed him. "Though I never told him plainly. I should hae, long ago."

"He's not the sort to understand the subtle approach," Ewan agreed. "Though it should be clear as day by now."

" 'Tis clear to him now," Rosalind assured him. "He just hasn't accepted it yet."

"Accepted what?" He knew what she meant but had an itch to hear her say the words aloud.

"That *you*"—her smile plainly told him she knew what he was up to and didn't mind humoring his whim—"are the only man I'm interested in courting."

&

"He's your brother," Rosalind grumbled to Marlene as Brent skated in circles around Ewan, edging closer in a blatant bid to make him uncomfortable. "Can't you do something?"

"They're competing over you," Marlene shot back. "And since when has my brother ever listened to a word I say—unless it's 'dinner'?" She watched as Ewan changed directions, leisurely skimming backwards while Brent continued his annoying tactics. "Nice footwork, there. If you ask me, I'd say Ewan can handle Brent without any assistance from either of us."

"Of course he can." Rosalind beamed with pride. "Ewan's handled far more than whatever ice tricks Brent can throw at him. I just wish. . ." her voice trailed off.

"You wish what?" Marlene did a neat turn and stop, narrowly avoiding Luke as he zoomed around the perimeter of the pond.

"That Brent hadn't invited himself along." Rosalind sighed. "Not that he doesn't have every right to come to the pond, but. . .this was supposed to be a fun outing. And now. . .well, you see." She gestured to where the two men had evidently decided to stage an impromptu race across the pond. "They're being. . ." She searched for a word other than *competitive* and came up short.

"Men?" Marlene zigzagged. "And you don't think it's even a tiny bit fun to have two men competing for your affection?"

"No!" Rosalind slid to a halt. "I'm not a prize at some country fair to be won by the man who can skate the fastest or eat the most pies in a single sitting. 'Tis pure foolishness, Marlene."

"Love makes fools out of us all, sooner or later." Marlene moved gently, leaving wavelike tracks in her wake as she circled Rosalind. "If a race or pie could bring Johnny back right now, I'd do it without thinking twice. But it's not so simple."

"No, it isn't." Rosalind reached out to clasp one of her friend's hands, and they skated side by side. "Here I am, going on about myself when my Ewan is scant paces away. Do you miss Johnny terribly, Marlene?" She gave a soft squeeze in sympathy.

"Part of me does," she admitted. "But I'm more worried about the part of me that's glad he went on with the railroad. I keep thinking that since he's gone now—when we'll be snowed in most of the time anyway—he'll be here in the spring. That's when we'll be able to see each other more. That's when he can start working the land he'll buy and building our house. If he stayed now, he'd be gone then. This way is best."

"Exactly!" Rosalind stared at her friend. "This is the way I knew you'd be once you'd thought it o'er."

"I did behave like the worst brat." Marlene flushed. "I'm blessed that you understood, Ewan forgave me, and Johnny wasn't scared away forever by my terrible temper!"

"You'll have to do far worse to frighten any of us away." Rosalind let go of Marlene's hand to do a quick spin. "We know what a wonderful woman lies beneath a passing mood. And in just a few short weeks, you've already unearthed her! Johnny will find an even better catch than he remembers when he comes back."

"I hope so—oof!" Marlene fell into Rosalind as Brent whizzed by too closely, throwing her off balance. Both girls crashed to the ice in an ungainly heap of arms and skirts and skates.

"Ooh," Rosalind moaned, rubbing the back of her head where it had met the ice so suddenly. "Are you all right, Marlene?" She disentangled her skates from her friend's and knelt beside her.

"Yes. I—I think so." She gingerly sat up, rubbing her elbow. "Just caught me off guard. Where is. . .Brent!" She glowered at her brother. "See what your showing off has done?"

As Ewan helped Rosalind, Brent yanked on Marlene's arms to pull her to her feet.

"I'll help!" Luke came speeding toward them, only to hit a slippery patch and come crashing down himself.

"Luke!" Rosalind pushed away from Ewan and raced to her brother's side. "Are you all right? Say something." Her brother's labored breathing chilled her in a way the hard ice and winter wind had not. "Let's get you back to the house."

"Knocked the wind out of you, did it?" Ewan lifted the small boy to his feet. "Well, I'd say we've done enough damage for one afternoon. Let's see if we can talk your mam into giving us some more of that wonderful mulled cider of hers." He led Luke to solid ground, and everyone unlaced their metal blades for the trek home.

Rosalind took care to walk slowly, leaving Ewan's side to hover around Luke. His flushed cheeks and continued coughing made her throat clench shut. *I was so busy worrying about myself and talking wi' Marlene, I didn't watch him closely enough. We should hae left before any o' this happened. 'Tis my fault he struggles so.*

Lord, please be wi' my brother. Put Your healing hand o'er him and help him to breathe. I'll sit him by the hearth and get him something warm to drink. Please don't let this episode worsen from my negligence, Father. His breath rasps and his chest heaves—please ease his breathing, Lord. Please.

Before they got to the house, her fervent prayers had been answered. While he still rasped, Luke's coughing had abated. She bundled him by the fire and gave him the first cup of hot cider, relaxing only when his faint wheeze was barely audible.

"Rosalind," Ewan spoke from behind her. "Why don't we walk Marlene and Brent home?"

"Of course." Rosalind shot him an apologetic smile. For a short time, she'd all but forgotten about everyone else!

The walk passed pleasantly enough, with Marlene and Brent soon ensconced in the Freimont house. Rosalind found herself suddenly alone with Ewan as they made their way back home.

Ewan waited until they were midway on the return to stop. "Rosalind, what's wrong?"

"Wrong?" Rosalind frowned. "Nothing. Marlene's seen the wisdom of Johnny's decision, neither of us suffered more than a bruise from the fall, and Luke's fine. What could be wrong?"

❧

"Go back to the part about Luke being fine. 'Tisn't usual for a sister to fuss so o'er a twelve-year-old boy." Ewan peered at Rosalind. "He's nearing manhood, by then."

At about that same age, I was taking care of Mam wi' my father gone on to America. I worked hard and checked for Da's letters every day, trying to fill his shoes and hold everything together.

"He fell, too," Rosalind reminded him, but the answer didn't satisfy. Her gaze wouldn't meet his completely.

"I know." Ewan tilted her chin toward him. "I can see for myself that Luke's small for his age—small enough not t' spend all his time at the forge. But I've never seen him there. And today, when a small tumble knocked the wind out o' him, he gasped for breath all the way back home. So I'll ask you again, Rosalind. . ." He paused meaningfully. "What is wrong?"

"Will you start to treat him differently if something is?" she hedged, her eyes searching his face intently. "Or will you continue to see him as a normal boy and not coddle him?"

"You coddle him enough for both of us, t' my way of thinking." He said it gently, but firmly enough to reassure her.

"Luke's never been strong." She pulled her chin from his grasp to hold his hand in hers. "He was born wi' weak lungs. The doctors say 'tis nothing short o' a miracle he survived past infancy. He can't abide the smoke o' the forge—that's why he doesn't work wi' Da. We don't speak on it, as it pains them both."

"I see." Ewan nodded. "And the cold? 'Tis the reason he coughed and you stopped the snowball fight?"

"Aye," she admitted. "He had an episode then. . .and again today. I keep close watch o'er him so they don't worsen, but today I wasn't careful enough. It could hae been much worse."

" 'Twasn't your fault that he fell, Rosalind."

"No, but he'd probably begun rasping afore that even." She looked down at the toes of her boots. "I should hae checked on him sooner. He will not admit when he's done too much."

"What happens when it worsens?" He pulled her closer, putting his arm about her waist.

"He coughs so hard his body is wracked wi' it. His chest heaves and he fights for breath until his face goes pale and his mouth turns blue. There's not a winter as goes by but he gets terribly ill. A simple cold sets him coughing, and it settles in his chest, and then"—the tears in her eyes when she looked up at him flooded his heart—"we all fight so he'll see the spring."

"Why didn't you tell me?" He cupped her cheek and used the pad of his thumb to wipe away her tears. "Let me help you."

"I didn't want you to treat him as though he were too fragile to do anything. He's a boy like any other and needs to laugh and play and feel useful. Luke brightens whenever you're around because you don't mollycoddle him." She bit her lip. "Da loves him and tries so hard to give him freedom tempered wi' safeguards, but Luke sees through it. I didn't want that for you or Luke."

"I understand." He took a deep breath. "And I'll treat him no differently. We'll leave it to you to shoo us back into the warmth of the house when you feel 'tis the right time."

"Thank you, Ewan." She rose on tiptoe to plant a soft kiss on his cheek.

He fought the urge to turn his head, knowing it wasn't the right time. Ewan settled for keeping his arm around her waist as they walked back to the house.

I may not be able to protect Rosalind from Luke's weakness, he reasoned, *but I can make it easier for her to look after him. A nice group we'll be. . .Rosalind watches o'er Luke, I'll watch o'er Rosalind, and God will watch o'er us all. May Christmas come to find us all hearty and full of joy.*

sixteen

" '. . .And the angel said unto them, Fear not: for, behold, I bring you good tidings of great joy, which shall be to all people.' " Da's voice rang with conviction as he read the Christmas story. " 'For unto you is born this day in the city of David a Savior, which is Christ the Lord. And this shall be a sign unto you; Ye shall find the babe wrapped in swaddling clothes, lying in a manger. And suddenly there was with the angel a multitude of heavenly host praising God, and saying, Glory to God in the highest, and on earth peace, good will toward men.' Luke, chapter 2, verses 10 to 14." He reverently shut the family Bible.

Rosalind blinked, trying to clear the tears from her eyes. The wonder of that scene—the majesty of a newborn king come to save all men.

Jesus, You are so good to us. You sacrificed Your splendor to be born a man, and we did not appreciate it. The Prince of Heaven offered a manger. Each time I hear the words, I marvel at Your greatness—the most powerful of all brought to us as a helpless babe. I struggle with pride, yet Your example shows the meaning of true humility. Thank You for Your loving grace, which brings us such undeserved joy.

Her tears stopped, and she found Ewan watching her, his own face shining with the light of love.

"We've so many blessings to be thankful for this Christmas," he said. "Christ's own love is mirrored at this hearth. 'Tis been many a year since I took part in such a celebration."

"We're glad to have you, Ewan." Rosalind stood and walked over to place a hand on his shoulder. His joy had been mixed with such wistfulness, she wanted to brush away the sorrow. "Shall we sing a few Christmas carols?"

" 'Tis been too long since I heard the Irish Christmas Carol." Ewan looked around hopefully. "Do you all know it?"

"Of course!" Luke hummed the tune. " 'Tis Grandmam's favorite."

"Aye, 'tis." Grandmam rocked back, smiling in remembrance and anticipation. "Why don't you start it for us, Mr. Gailbraith?"

"I'd be honored." Ewan cleared his throat and broke into the melody, his rich baritone flowing over the words as everyone joined in.

> *Christmas day is come; let's all prepare for mirth,*
> *Which fills the heav'ns and earth at this amazing birth.*
> *Through both the joyous angels in strife and hurry fly,*
> *with glory and hosannas, 'All Holy' do they cry. . ."*

Rosalind closed her eyes and let the song wash over her. *My family is well, Ewan is wi' us, and we're celebrating the Lord's birth. What could be better?*

When the final note quavered in the air, she opened her eyes. "Any other favorites?"

And so they praised the night away, singing beloved hymns such as "O Come, All Ye Faithful," "Angels, from the Realms of Glory," and "Joy to the World."

When the candles guttered, eyelids drooped, and stomachs groaned with satisfaction, Ewan rose from the settle. "Will you walk wi' me a wee while?"

Rosalind looked to Da for permission. At his short nod, she swirled her thick cloak over her shoulders and stepped into the thick night with Ewan. Only a single candle and the light from the heavens illuminated their path. Rosalind could see her breaths coming in little white puffs of the frigid night air as he pulled her close.

"Ewan, why are we stopping?" Rosalind stamped her feet to warm them as he set the candle on a sturdy log and took both her hands in his own. A curious warmth suddenly took away the chill.

"Rosalind," he began, "there is an old Irish marriage blessing. Do you know it?"

"Nay." Rosalind fixed her gaze upon him, understanding his purpose in bringing her outside. They were alone, under the stars, and he spoke of marriage!

She didn't dare breathe as he recited the blessing:

"May God be wi' you and bless you.
   May you see your children's children.
May you be poor in misfortunes
   and rich in blessings.
May you know nothing but happiness
   from this day forward."

He paused, giving her time to savor the sweetness of the words. "Rosalind, God has blessed me simply by letting me know you." He sank to his knees, still clasping her hands. "I love you. Will you make me rich in His blessings and bring me even more happiness by saying you'll wed me?"

Tears streaked down her face as Rosalind let out the breath she'd been holding to kneel in front of him. "Yes, Ewan. Oh, yes!" She threw her arms around him and sank into his warm embrace as his lips sought her own.

He pulled away a short while later and fumbled in his coat pocket. "Here." He held up a small, carved box, dwarfed by his palm.

Rosalind took it and opened the lid to find a simple gold band inside. She gasped as he drew it out and slid it onto her left ring finger.

" 'Twas my mother's." His hoarse whisper made her realize his eyes shone with unshed tears. " 'Tis all I hae left o' her, and I know she'd smile to see the beautiful bride I've given it to."

"And I'm proud to wear it," she whispered. "I love you, Ewan Gailbraith."

seventeen

"Still no word as to when the circuit rider will pass through?" Ewan worked to clear underbrush and rotten logs from around the bases of the sugar maples.

"None. 'Twas a harsh winter, so 'tisn't surprising." Arthur grinned. "Probably settled in somewhere to wait it out. Don't worry. Now that 'tis warm enough for the sap to run, he'll turn up."

"Good." Ewan carried a load of dead brush over to where they'd have the boiling place.

Lord, winter begins to change to spring, and still Rosalind is naught but my intended! Close to three months now, I've waited as patiently as I can. I'm anxious to make her my bride in truth, though I see the wisdom in Your timing. I've yet to determine where I'll set up household wi' my Rosalind. If I stay, I'll take Arthur's livelihood. Should I go, I separate her from the family I've come to love as well.

"Hold a moment, son." Arthur put a hand on Ewan's forearm, halting him. "I wanted a word wi' you. I know you want to be wed, and we've both been praying o'er where you'll settle. But I was wondering whether you're any closer to a decision?"

"I don't want to take Rosalind away from Saddleback," Ewan stated flatly before softening. "To tell the truth, I don't want to leave, myself. And yet, should I stay. . ." He let the thought hang, unable to speak of the harsh reality to the man who'd been so kind.

"You're worried you'll take away my customers." Arthur nodded. "I surmised as much when you asked my blessing. Hae you any solution to the problem?"

Ewan straightened his shoulders. "I've thought I might turn my hand to farming. I've a solid bit of money tucked away, more than I'd need for a good while. 'Twould do to seed a new spread, and I'm used to working wi' my hands."

"You're a blacksmith, son." Arthur clapped a hand on his shoulder, frowning. " 'Twouldn't do to try to change who you are."

For the first time, Ewan noted how the fine lines about the older man's mouth and eyes had deepened. Was it merely the strain of winter, or something else?

"I'm not a young man anymore." Arthur rubbed the back of his neck. "And I'm starting to feel my age. The cold brings a stiffness to my fingers and a tightness to my chest."

"I see." And Ewan could see what it cost the great man to admit it. "Wi' spring coming, that 'twill ease."

"Aye, for a while. But each year the stiffness hae lingered a bit longer, and the twinges hae turned to steady aches." Arthur looked ruefully at his strong hands. "I've seen forty-five years, Ewan. At this age, I'd thought to have a son beside me at the forge, taking on the lion's share o' the work."

Ewan glanced back to where Luke snapped dead branches a ways off. He looked back to Arthur. They both knew Luke wouldn't be the help to his father's business that Arthur had hoped for.

"Aye, you see what I'm saying. Kaitlin and I lost two babes between Rose and Luke—one too soon to tell whether the child was a lad or lassie, and one boy. Our James didna live to see his second year." Arthur's eyes burned with a fierce light.

"And we both know Luke isna fit for smithing, and I won't hae him risking his life to try. I'll not lose my son to pride."

Not knowing what to say, Ewan simply nodded. He waited and listened, fighting not to compare Arthur with his own father. He'd begun to see where Arthur was heading with this conversation.

"Now the Lord hae seen fit to bring a fine man to my doorstep, who's won my Rosey's heart and hae proven himself a man of his word." Arthur paused. "And he's a blacksmith wi' no forge to call his own and loathe to take my daughter far from our family. 'Tis no stretch to see God's hand in this.

"I make a good living here, and wi' the railroad tracks laid, more business will be passing through than a lone old man can handle. Ewan, I'd be honored if you'd work by my side at the forge."

For a moment, Ewan couldn't speak, choked by an avalanche of thoughts. *I knew 'twas my lot to ever bear the burden of my poor decision. My da turned his back on me when I'd not yet reached the age o' sixteen. In all the years since he went to America, I've not laid eyes on the man, though I've tried to track him down.*

Now here's a man not bound to me by blood, calling me "son" and asking me to stand alongside him.

"I'm the one who's honored, Arthur." Ewan embraced his father-in-law-to-be with a hearty slap on the back. "Though you're no old man yet. You've a need for grandchildren before you claim that title."

"And that's another joy you'll be bringing me." Arthur stepped back. "I've high expectations," he warned.

Ewan grinned. "I plan to meet every one."

❧

"Do you know what you'll do when the circuit riding preacher finally does arrive?" Marlene drove a spike into one of the sugar maples. "Or has Ewan still said nothing about whether you'll stay in Saddleback or not? I pray you'll stay!"

"He's mentioned trying his hand at farming," Rosalind answered. "I think he fears taking away Da's business if he opens his smithy here, but neither of us wants to move very far."

"What happened to all your great dreams of travel?" Marlene stepped back as Rosalind pushed a trough into place beneath the hollow tube. "You've always said you want to see the world beyond our small corner of it. Not that I'm complaining if you're choosing to stay here with us, mind."

"I still do." Rosalind moved to the next tree with a cleared base. "Wi' the railroad tracks already laid, trains will start passing through. Ewan and I will hae the freedom to hop aboard whenever—and to wherever—we please and be back more quickly than I ever dreamed. Besides"—she gave a small smile—"I'm thinking marriage might be enough of an adventure to last a short while, at least. My own house will offer quite a change."

"Most likely," Marlene agreed. "I know I can't wait for mine! With spring upon us, my Johnny should be coming back any day." She peered about as though half expecting to see him pop out from behind the tree she just finished tapping.

"Or it could be a month," Rosalind gently reminded. Seeing the shadow creeping over her friend's face, she quickly changed the subject. "And what of Johnny? Will Da have to expect competition from your beau?" She said it lightly but couldn't hide the tinge of concern she felt. *Da, Ewan, and Johnny? 'Tis two too many blacksmiths for a single town, even wi' the railroad trade.*

"Oh, no." Marlene brushed her concerns aside and tripped

over to the next tree. "Johnny doesn't actually like smithing. Says it's hot, dirty, and loud. He'd prefer to be a wainwright, just working on wheels. I'm glad I won't be washing soot from his shirts every week! Does that put your mind at ease?"

"Yes." Rosalind didn't pretend not to know what Marlene meant. "Mayhap Da will be the blacksmith, Ewan the farrier, and Johnny the wainwright as Saddleback grows larger. The railroad will bring people. Our skilled menfolk will keep them nearby."

"That's a thought." Marlene handed the auger to Rosalind. "Of course, Johnny needs to come back and the preacher needs to show up before any of those plans will bear fruit!"

"Parson Burchill always had a fondness for maple sweeties." Rosalind moved on to the final tree in the immediate area. "Wi' the lure of those along wi' the welcome of warmer days, he'll turn up soon." She stepped back to survey her work. "I hope."

Talk turned to their hope chests as the girls made their way back to the sugaring-off shelter. They found everyone congregated there, waiting for the wooden troughs to fill.

The Twadleys, Horntons, and Prestons would be tapping trees nearer to home, so only a few households were represented out here. The MacLeans; Ewan; Marlene's parents; Brent, of course; and Marlene's uncles, Jakob and Isaac Albright, with their mail-order brides; made up the work crew. Grandmam sat bundled by the boiling fire, overseeing everything to her heart's content. Fourteen neighbors welcoming spring and greeting each other after a long winter of snowy solitude— the sugar they'd make this day only sweetened the cheerful meeting.

They snacked on cold biscuits and cheese, chatting about

anything and everything until it was time to get to work. The sap ran from the trunks in thick, gooey streams. As the hollowed troughs filled, everyone took care to replace them with empty ones and pour the bounty into buckets. The first troughs filled always made the very best sugar, so they boiled separately.

"Amazing how the ants always appear, isn't it?" Marlene brushed a few of the insects away, saving them from drowning in the sap. "And they never learn that the sap will kill them."

"Don't worry. You know the milk foam will bring all the bugs and bits o'bark to the top, and we'll skim it out," Rosalind teased. She knew that was Marlene's least favorite part of the sugaring.

"I remember," her friend spoke flatly. "Better out with the foam than floating in my syrup, though." She gave a shudder.

They hauled full buckets back to the boiling fire, handing them off to their mothers and Luke, who watched the sap boil with eagle eyes as it separated into syrup and sugar. A smaller pot hung with the other large ones, promising a special treat.

Everyone took turns emptying troughs, filling buckets, watching the boiling sap, and shooing away greedy squirrels and dogs that crept close enough to pose a threat. Humans weren't the only ones who had a taste for something sweet every now and again.

" 'Tis hard work," Ewan commented. "Though the rewards will be sweet enough to merit it. I'd not thought the animals would cause problems. Shouldn't the fire and noise scare them away?"

"You'd think." Rosalind walked with him to the farthest sugar maples to check the troughs. "But there're actually stories about livestock trying to steal a taste." She caught his disbelieving look.

"Really! There's an old tale about a prize bull named Prince who popped his head into one of his owner's tins of hot sugar. The heat shocked him so that he ran off wi' the best of the batch stuck all around his muzzle, and the cows followed!"

"There's a yarn, to be sure." Ewan shook his head. "Though I don't doubt you believe 'tis the truth, Rosalind."

"What?" She stopped dead in her tracks. "You think that I'm easily taken in by false stories, do you now, Ewan Gailbraith?"

"No." He held up his hands in mute apology. "I just meant that you wouldn't knowingly pass on an untruth. You've too strong a character for something like that. 'Twas a compliment!"

"From the man who tells stories of conductors wi' bears and three-man-hunts for a solitary lost railroad spike." She shook her head. "They're naught but tales told to teach us."

"And what is the story of the bull and the maple sugar supposed to teach us?" Ewan folded his arms across his chest.

"To keep close watch o'er the things we value," Rosalind explained, "lest someone more daring come and take it away."

"In that case"—laughing, he swept her into his arms—"I suppose I should just keep a tight hold on you. Even though it seems Brent has accepted our engagement, I'd rather be careful."

"Ewan!" She reluctantly pushed away. "We've work to be doing. Now isn't the time to be stealing kisses—wi' half the town only paces away!" She moved to pick up the dropped bucket.

"Seems like the perfect time." He stepped close once more. He lowered his head and whispered in her ear, "After all, we're harvesting sweets today." With that, he pressed his lips to hers in a fleeting caress before swiping the bucket from her.

"You're incorrigible," she said, the sting of the reprimand

stolen by her flushed cheeks and gentle smile.

"I'm in love," he corrected, sweeping her hand into his. "And in the mood to celebrate. Your da has asked me to work alongside him at the smithy. I'll not need to forsake my trade to turn my hands to a plow nor move us from Saddleback."

"Oh, Ewan!" This time she threw her arms around him. "Why didn't you say so sooner? This is wonderful news—just perfect!"

"And so"—he planted a swift peck on her nose—"are you."

"I hate to disappoint," she warned, "but no one's perfect."

eighteen

"I hate to say it, Rosalind, but you were right." Ewan sat heavily on a log placed by the fire for that purpose. "You're not quite perfect, after all." He shook his head.

"I know," she responded, looking puzzled. "But what, in particular, has made you change your mind so very quickly?"

"How can you like this better than the corn husking?" He winked. "I happen to have some very fond memories of that day." His roundabout mention of their first kiss made her blush that delightful pink shade he'd come to be so fond of.

"'Tis harder work than the corn husking," she admitted, not taking the bait. "And 'tis far colder, too, but my favorite part of the day is coming up now. You'll change your mind back soon."

"I look forward to it." He gave a mighty stretch.

"You'll need this." She handed him a small wooden spoon with a rather long handle. "And you'll want to follow me." He watched as she took the last pot left on the fire—the smaller one that's sap had boiled down to a sludge-like syrup—and walked around the shanty and out of sight.

He hurried to his feet and followed, finding everyone eagerly crowding around Rosalind and her still-hot pot—each of them brandishing one of the curious wooden spoons like his. He watched as she set the pot on a sturdy old tree stump and backed away until she stood beside him.

Together, they watched as first Luke, then everyone else,

dipped a spoonful of the thick syrup and hurried away, dropping the contents on a patch of hard snow a little ways off. Luke picked up his newly hardened piece almost right away and bit into it, his eyes closed with obvious enjoyment as he swallowed.

"This is the sugaring-off." Rosalind nudged him forward. "Go ahead—they'll all keep coming back for more until there's none left at all. Believe me, you'll want to try some for yourself."

Shrugging, Ewan stepped forward, waited for Luke to scurry away with his third helping, and loaded his own spoon with the hot, gloppy brown mixture. He went back to where Rosalind waited with her own portion and mimicked her as she flipped the syrup onto the hard-packed snow.

Almost immediately, the syrup froze into a hardened disk. Ewan picked it up and bit into the crunchy sweet that's cold flavor melted on his tongue. He started walking back to the pot before he finished the last bite of his first taste of the treat. He ignored Rosalind's laughter as he returned to her side with a heaping spoonful of the goop and eagerly flipped it onto the snow. He couldn't ignore her when she snatched his sweet from right under his nose.

"Thank you, sweetheart." She bit into it with relish. "So thoughtful of you to fetch more for me. Very gentlemanly!" she called as he tromped off once again to scrape the last spoonful from the very bottom of the pot as everyone watched.

Everyone but Arthur and his wife. Ewan noticed that Arthur began coughing as the day wore on and kept putting his hand to his head, as though in pain. He'd seen Mrs. MacLean rubbing her husband's temples to comfort him, but he grew pale.

"Mam and Da are going home." Rosalind pinched the folds of her skirts. "Da has a headache he says is worsening. I heard him coughing. . . . I hope he isn't taking ill. Perhaps some extra rest will do the trick, and that's why Mam is taking him home for now. I'll need to keep a close eye on Luke. The days are warmer, but the nights bring a harsh chill as the sun sets."

"You're good to care so." He led her toward the fire. "And we're finishing up the boiling. 'Twill be done soon."

After the work ended, they all gathered around the fire in the waning light to share stories and laughter. Rosalind prevailed upon Ewan to tell more of his railroad legends, and he had to search his memory to find one worthy of the occasion.

"Ah. I'll tell about Mr. Villard's special train."

"Mr. Villard? The railroad owner who ran the Last Spike ceremony?" Jakob Albright frowned.

"The same one. And funny enough, this story—which has been sworn to me as true—takes place on the ride up to Independence Creek for that very ceremony." Ewan paused for effect, watching to see that he had everyone's attention before he began.

"Well, Mr. Villard brought his wife, their babe, and the babe's nurse along to be a part of his triumph. After a stop in St. Paul, Mrs. Villard made the appalling discovery that all the babe's linens were soiled—there were none clean in the hamper. Obviously, this just would not do. She notified her husband of the problem."

"Seems to me," Marlene's father, Dustin, commented, "that they should have packed enough of the linens to begin with."

"Or been responsible enough to do a wash," harrumphed Delana Freimont. "You'd think between the mother and the nurse, one of the two would have taken care of the matter long before."

"Aye," Ewan agreed. "But the fact of the matter was that they were stopped in St. Paul wi' naught but a hamper full o' soiled linen. Mr. Villard ordered the hamper be rushed to the Pullman laundry service, where it would be washed and returned before the train even pulled out of St. Paul."

"'Tis good to own a railroad, I see," Gilda cackled. "To have your high and mighty wife send her laundry to the workers!"

"Now, I never met Mrs. Villard personally, mind," Ewan continued, "so I can't speak as to how hoity-toity a miss she may or may not hae been. But whichever the case, as the train made its way toward Helena, the distraught nurse came before her mistress and whispered that the hamper was nowhere on board. The whole thing had been left behind in St. Paul after all."

Ewan noted that Luke slipped away from the fire, and, after a short while, Rosalind followed after him. Unwilling to draw attention to their absence, he finished the railroad legend.

"So Mr. Villard ordered that an engine and car should be found immediately and made to follow their train at all speed to bring his wife the hamper of linens. And so the special train, not weighted by a heavy load, sped o'er the tracks and managed to overtake the Villard family before they reached Helena.

"Flushed wi' the triumph of his idea, Villard watched the gleeful nurse open the hamper...and find naught but the same soiled linens."

Gasps and laughter sounded around the fire as everyone speculated on who Mr. Villard blamed for the entire affair and what they ever did about the baby. Who could imagine a special train sent to fetch a baby's laundry—and that laundry not done?

Ewan, for his part, searched the darkness beyond the perimeter of the fire, trying to find Rosalind and Luke. As they still did not appear, a frisson of tension shot down his spine. *After such a fine day, surely nothing is wrong?*

ᔰ

Something was very wrong. Rosalind could feel the unease as a palpable thing while she searched for her younger brother.

"Luke!" She whispered, at first, loathe to make a scene and embarrass him. Holding her lantern aloft to better see her way, she kept on. Darkness pressed in around the modest light, throwing shadows wherever she turned. "Luke!" she called more loudly after he still had not answered.

He knew better than to wander off into the woods alone—especially in the dark. He could fall or find himself in a much worse predicament. After a harsh winter, predators would be more aggressive. Luke should still be within earshot, but Rosalind heard no answering call to soothe her frayed nerves.

Lord, there are dangers out in the wild, but Luke faces even more. 'Tis growing colder by the moment. I've not checked in on him since before the sugaring-off. Please, do not let him be in trouble. For the first time in my memory, Luke's made it through the winter wi'out a severe illness. Now that spring is upon us, 'twould be cruel for his weakness to sicken him. Guide my footsteps and help me find my brother. Let him be safe.

"Luke!" Praying fervently between calls, she stopped and listened. There it was—the shallow rasp of Luke's breathing. She turned toward the sound, her lantern's light showing her brother sitting on the cold ground, his back against a tree.

"Rose." He gave a game smile. "I'm all right." But the words came out hard and fast—forced.

"No, you're not." She knelt beside him and threw her cloak

around them both. *I've heard him speak like this afore—when he's holding his breath, trying to push back the coughing.* "Don't fight it, Luke. 'Twill go easier if you don't try to hold it back." She stood, pulling him to his feet.

Guided by the lantern light, she kept a slow pace, careful not to overexert him. He coughed and rasped and coughed in spite of her best efforts. Luke needed to be where the air was warm and where she could get a hot drink down him to ease his throat and breathing.

"When did the tightness begin?" She kept her voice steady, not accusing or angry or frightened. "How long?"

"The sugaring-off." His words ended in a horrible hacking that shook his entire frame.

Of course. Breathing in the cold air, then hurrying to eat frozen sweets would bring this on. And I was too wrapped up in Ewan to think of it. I didn't watch Luke as closely as I should.

"Why did you not say so?" Rosalind couldn't bite back the question. *Did it seem I would not care if he needed my help?*

"I didn't—" Coughs interrupted his answer, and they stopped mere yards away from the boiling fire. Finally, they subsided. "I didn't want to miss any of the fun. And"—he glanced sideways at her—"I didn't want you to miss any of it either."

"There will always be opportunities for fun!" She hugged him tight around the shoulders as they kept walking "Don't you know that you're more important than any combination of sweets and stories? You're my brother and you always come first."

"Sorry." The piteous mumble wrung her heartstrings as they stepped into the flickering light of the big fire.

"Rosalind! Luke!" Ewan hurried over to greet them. "We were beginning to worry about you." He hunkered down to peer at Luke. One look obviously told him her brother wasn't well, because he scooped the boy into his arms before addressing everyone.

" 'Tis been a long day, and I'm as tuckered as Luke, here." He spoke loudly enough to hide the sound of the boy's ragged breathing. "So I'll be taking Rosalind home, now. We wish you all a pleasant night. I hope t' see you again soon."

With Rosalind's nod, he started out. She carried the lantern; he carried the more precious cargo. Even nestled against Ewan's warmth, Luke's coughing grew steadily worse before they reached the house.

"Mam!" Rosalind pushed open the door and rushed inside, dragging a chair as close to the roaring hearth fire as she dared. She hurried to put on a kettle of water while Ewan deposited Luke in the chair.

Mam took one look at her son's pale face, heard the labored breathing, and pulled out a warm quilt to wrap around him. She pulled off his gloves, chafing his hands as she knelt at his side. "How long has he been this way?" Her question sent another pang of guilt through Rosalind as she brewed the tea.

"He says his chest started feeling tight after the sugaring-off." Rosalind spoke for Luke, as he fought for breath. She scooped out some of the eucalyptus leaves and peppermint that had always helped to ease his coughing before and prayerfully would again.

"Why didn't he come wi' us when his da felt poorly?" Mam's face fell. "I should hae checked on him afore I took your father off." She smoothed back Luke's hair. "I'm sorry, son."

"No." Rosalind choked on the words as she finally handed over a mug of steaming tea. " 'Tis my fault. You left him in my care, but I didn't realize aught was amiss until he left the fire and did not immediately return to join us." She bowed her head. "I went after him and found him trying to stop the coughing."

"You weren't holding it in, were you?" Mam turned a harsh gaze on Luke as he breathed in the warm steam from his mug. At his sheepish nod, she sighed. "That always makes it worse."

"Aye." Rosalind sat wearily on the settle, beside Ewan. "As I brought him back to the fire, and then on to home, he worsened."

" 'Tis true." Ewan frowned. "I carried the lad and could feel it as he found it harder and harder to draw breath."

"You did what you could." Mam sat back on her heels. "Thank you, Ewan, for helping Rose bring him home. Now we keep him warm and propped up, and hope that 'twill pass quickly."

Please, Father, Rosalind prayed as Ewan took his leave. *Please let this be a short episode. Do not let him worsen but instead feel better. Let Luke be well again come morning. Amen.*

nineteen

Four mornings later, Ewan knocked on the MacLean door, carrying a brace of freshly caught rabbits. *Wi' Arthur and Luke on the mend, nothing will go down half so good as hot rabbit stew— best thing to bring a man back to his feet.* When Rosalind, eyes heavy with dark circles, opened the door, his smile vanished.

"What's happened?" He shouldered past her, dropping the skinned game atop the wooden table. An unnatural stillness filled the house for a brief moment before both Arthur and Luke broke into coughing spasms, the sound shattering the silence.

"They were doing better." Rosalind's voice came in an exhausted whisper. "It seemed as though they were on their way to recovery just yesterday. But come nightfall. . ."

"Fever came upon them both." Gilda, rocking more erratically than Ewan had ever seen, spoke up. "Their breathing labored. . .the coughing wracks their bodies. Nothing helps."

Ewan sat heavily on the settle, running a hand over his face. For two days after he'd carried Luke home, Rosalind and Kaitlin had tended to Arthur and Luke night and day. Only yesterday it had seemed they'd turned the corner and the worst of it had passed. But now. . . He stared helplessly to where Rosalind stooped by Luke, propping him up on cushions to ease his breathing.

"When they're more upright, they take in more air," she explained as she noticed him watching. "That and the heat and the tea are all we can do for them. Mam's asleep now after staying up all night. They were improving—" She broke off in a stifled sob that wrung Ewan's heart.

He walked over to where she slumped by the hearth and fell to his knees. With his arms wrapped around her, her weary head nestled against his shoulders, she wept. Ewan prayed.

Lord, put Your hand on this home and Your children wi'in it. Bring healing to Arthur, ease to Luke's lungs, and rest to the women who've worn themselves weak with worry. This illness is more than we alone can handle, Father. We turn to Your wisdom and mercy, and seek Your blessings upon those we hold dear.

He stroked the soft strands of Rosalind's hair that had come free from her braid over the long night. He listened as her sobs quieted, until her breathing came long and deep in the even cadence of sleep. He shifted slowly, so as not to wake her. He swept her into his arms in one smooth motion and looked up at the loft ladder, where her bed must be.

I dare not climb it wi' her in my arms. Even were there no danger of bumping her head or worse, I'd not risk waking her.

"When she wakes, she'll take pains not to close her eyes for a scant moment, lest she sleep again," Gilda warned. "Lay her on the settle, so she can catch whatever rest she's able. Poor lass hae worn herself to a frazzle, helping her mam tend everyone these past days. The false hopes o' yesterday stole what strength she had left." The old woman kept rocking, her gaze flitting from one family member to the next in an unceasing vigil.

Ewan nodded, easing Rosalind down onto the furniture so gently she scarcely stirred. He pulled a crocheted afghan over her to keep her as comfortable as possible. That done, he stood, trying to think of ways he could help her—help them all.

Heavenly Father, when I was a wee lad, I caught ill in such a way. Mam did all the things Kaitlin and Rosalind have already seen to, but something tickles the edges of my memory—a warmth pressed to my chest, the strong smell making my eyes water. What kind of poultice did she use when all else failed to make me well? What made me feel better, though I disliked it? I remember thinking I'd never get rid of the smell. . .of what? What was that scent?

He looked at the shelves full of baking supplies, spices, teas, and herbal remedies. Nothing fit the memory. Ewan paced back and forth—from the hearth, to the table, and back again—keeping his distance from Rosalind for fear he'd wake her with his heavy tread. He passed the kettle, the pot, the skinned rabbits, and the door to the root cellar more times than he could count, vainly trying to recall Mam's treatment.

Hearth. . .rocker. . .table. . .root cellar door. Luke beside the hearth, stirring with fever. The rhythmic rocking of Gilda's concern. The scrubbed wooden surface of the table. The metal ring of the root cellar door—*the root cellar!*

He grasped the metal ring and heaved upward, descending into the cool darkness beneath without stopping to grab a candle. Without a light, he groped around, searching for the answer that had plagued him all morning.

There. Ewan's hands closed around the burlap sack and he followed the light back into the warmth of the house. He cautiously shut the cellar door, mindful not only of Rosalind's sleep but of Gilda's avidly curious gaze.

"Onions?" She peered in disbelief as he shook some onto the table. "You had a sudden hankering for onions, of all things?"

"I remembered an old remedy my mother used when I was young an' fought to breathe." He grabbed a knife and began chopping the pungent bulbs. "I could only recall the strength of the scent—how much I disliked it—but that it worked. She chopped onions, boiled them down, and wrapped the mash in flannel. Than she placed the hot poultice on my chest, changing it out for new whenever the old one cooled." Ewan kept his voice low even as he chopped. " 'Twas the only thing that finally worked. I thought it might do the same for Arthur and Luke. They'll reek of the stuff for what seems like ages, but 'tis more than worth it."

"Aye." Gilda's rocker gave a final, protesting *creak* as she got to her feet. "I'll put some water on to boil and then help you. If they must be replaced when they cool, we'll need a great many of those onions." She worked as she whispered, and Ewan slid the first batch of chopped pieces into the heating water.

The two of them worked quietly, the only sounds the soft bubbling of the onions, the *snick* of their knives, and under it all, the horrible rattling gasps as Luke tried to breathe.

⁊ₐ

Rosalind lifted her head from the settle, blinking to find herself there. *How did I . . . Oh no, I must have fallen asleep!* Yet another instance of her failing to take proper care of Luke, and now her da. She swung her feet to the floor, tossing the afghan over the back of the settle.

"I didn't mean to fall asleep." She bustled over to where Luke lay, half propped up on a mound of pillows. "You should hae woken me." She looked pointedly at Ewan. "You know that."

"Aye." He plopped a steaming poultice on Luke's heat-pinkened chest. "I knew you'd want me to hae woken you. 'Tis why I didn't." With maddening calmness, he took another poultice to where Da lay on the great bed and changed it out.

"What are those?" Rosalind wrinkled her nose as she processed the pungent odor rising from the flannel packs. "Onions?"

"Aye." Grandmam stirred a pot. "Your Ewan remembered a remedy his mam used when he was but a lad."

"To a certain point." Ewan gave a wry grin. "I knew she made a smelly poultice, which eased the ache in my chest, but try as I might, I couldn't recall what she put in it."

"Lad near wore out the floorboards, pacing around while he tried to recollect what the mystery ingredient was. Finally, he looked at the root cellar door and remembered 'twas onions."

"I'd never hae thought to boil onions to ease a cough." Rosalind felt Luke's forehead with the back of her hand. "He's still o'er-warm." She cast a concerned glance over at Da, wondering whether the onions had wrought any effect on his symptoms.

"Arthur's taken well to it," Grandmam answered Rosalind's unspoken question. "He's stopped coughing, at least."

"Praise the Lord for that," Rosalind whispered, relieved that at least one of them was improving. Perhaps the onion treatment would eventually aid Luke as well. She looked to where he lay, half reclining, his breaths shallow and raspy. . . . No. She bent closer, listening intently.

No. Please, let me be wrong, she prayed, even as the ominous rattle came again. Luke fought not only tightness—there was fluid gathering in his lungs. With each breath, the rattling gurgle gave hideous warning. Rosalind dropped down, putting her arms about her brother and holding him close. *Come on, Luke. Fight it. Just keep breathing. Let the poultice do its work.*

Jesus, please, help him. This is as bad as he's ever been. His chest and ribs ache from the coughing. His head pounds wi' it. Only in this uneasy sleep does he find any respite. 'Tis grateful I am that Da begins to recover, but what of my brother? He's never been hardy— he can't take a prolonged illness. The tears she thought long shed came slipping to the surface once more as she battled for her brother the only way she knew how—on her knees. Prayer was the most powerful tool she could wield, if it served the Lord's purpose to grant her request. *If 'twasn't the Lord's will. . .* That didn't even bear thinking on.

Father, 'tis my negligence that is to blame. I should hae checked on him, watched him more closely. I should hae made him sip more broth and tea to ease his throat. I should never hae allowed myself to fall asleep when he needed me. Lord, don't let Luke suffer for my failings. Please, make him well. Let Ewan's treatment work for Luke as it has for Da. Please, Lord. Please. . .

The shrill of a steam whistle broke through her thoughts. Startled, she looked up to see Ewan bolt out the door, leaving his coat and hat behind as he raced off into the distance. He was heading for the train tracks.

❧

Please, Lord. Don't let me be too late. Let the train stop. 'Tis the answer we've all been praying for—the train can bring Luke to the doctor at Fort Benton where a wagon through the cold could not. Let me be on time.

He ran faster than he'd ever imagined—not for his life, but for Luke's. Ewan pictured Rosalind's tired face, the bruised-looking circles around her eyes, and pushed himself even harder. He rounded the smithy and found the train—already stopped.

Thank You, Father.

Ewan rushed aboard to have a short conversation with the engineer, a man by the name of Brody whom he'd worked with before.

"Brody, I've a sick little boy not far off who needs the care o' a real doctor. Will you wait a very short while so I can fetch him? 'Tis a matter o' life and death." Ewan didn't take a breath until he'd gotten through all of his request.

"We'll wait." Brody shook Ewan's hand. "I'm glad to see the railroad put to such worthy use. We've only stopped now to let off Johnny Mathers. Go on, now. Get the boy."

God's timing. Ewan didn't even stay to look for Johnny, instead rushing back to the MacLean household. When he stormed through the door, Rosalind stared in cautious hope.

"They're holding the train for Luke." Ewan began grabbing the boy's coat off the peg by the door. "The railroad will get him to Fort Benton—and the doctor—when he wouldn't make it on the long wagon ride. Arthur, Kaitlin?" He strode over to the bed, waking them both. "The train is waiting to take Luke to Fort Benton. He needs a doctor's care. Will you trust me to look after your son?"

"Aye." Arthur nodded weakly. "Though one of us should go."

"Rose will go." Gilda stood up. "I'm too old to start a new journey, and Kaitlin should stay to help keep you on the mend."

"Aye, Rosalind should go," Kaitlin said, though Ewan could tell she was torn between staying with her husband and going with her son—any mother's greatest dilemma.

"I'm ready." Rosalind held a valise in one arm and her cloak in the other. "I've packed tea and blankets and socks...everything I can think of to keep him comfortable on the journey. If 'tis settled, we need to go before the engineer changes his mind and sticks to his schedule."

"That's my girl." Ewan scooped Luke into his arms and strode toward her. "We'll be back before you know it. I give you my word."

"Godspeed!" Kaitlin called with a break in her voice. "We'll be in constant prayer."

With that, Ewan and Rosalind hurried out the door and toward the waiting train—their last chance to help Luke. Ewan didn't relax until they were on the train, steaming toward Benton at full speed.

They spoke little during the journey. Rosalind kept anxious eyes on her brother, propping him up and giving him sips of water as he slipped in and out of consciousness.

Ewan repeated a litany of prayer. *Thank You, Jesus, for sending the train. Let it not be too late. Work through the doctor in Benton to heal our Luke. . . .*

If asked, Ewan wouldn't have been able to say how long they spent on the train, only that it seemed much longer than it probably actually was. When they arrived, he tipped a porter to go fetch the doctor.

"He'll be all right now." Rosalind spoke words of hope, but her face was drawn with concern as she mopped Luke's brow. "He has to be."

"Hello?" A man clambered into the car with them, lugging a physician's bag. "I'm Dr. Carmichael. This must be the boy." Wasting no time, he knelt beside Luke.

Ewan and Rosalind watched with bated breath as he checked for fever and listened to Luke's breathing and heartbeat. The doctor's ruddy face grew long, his eyes dulling behind the round spectacles perched on his nose.

"I'm afraid it's not good news." Dr. Carmichael sat back, shoving his spectacles higher. "His fever is quite high and, I'd guess, has been for some time." He waited for Rosalind's despairing nod before continuing to share his assessment. "The cough has settled in his chest—pneumonia."

"What can we do?" Ewan strove to remain calm and find how best to serve Luke. "How do we help him now?"

"Make him as comfortable as possible. Keep him propped up, give him hot fluids, and make sure he's warm." Dr. Carmichael looked defeated as he spoke the words.

"We've done all that." Rosalind spoke in desperation. "We've been doing it since he first fell ill. Is there nothing else?"

"The only other thing I'm sure you've already been doing." The doctor looked from one face to another. "Pray."

twenty

"Is there no hope?" Rosalind turned to Ewan as the doctor left.

"Only if 'tis the Lord's will." His bleak stare offered little of the comfort she sought, though he reached out to take her hand in his. "Though I'll not pretend to understand it."

"No." A dry sob escaped her. "God won't take him away from us. We need him. God won't give us more sorrow than we can bear. Surely not. Luke!" She shook him, alarmed at how light he felt in her arms. "Luke!" Rosalind called louder, trying to rouse him where the doctor had failed. "Come on. Open your eyes."

His pale face seemed even more drawn, the dreaded tinge of blue creeping into his lips to steal him further away from her.

"Lucas Mathias MacLean," she ordered, ignoring the way her voice shook, "wake up this instant. Do you hear me, Luke? Open your eyes." She jostled him slightly.

"Rosalind," Ewan began, but her fierce glare silenced him.

"No. He'll listen. He'll wake up." She cupped Luke's face in her hands. "He's not so warm anymore. Maybe the fever is breaking." The blue tinge deepened, and his breathing grew shallow. "No. Wake up, Luke. You have to wake up." The whispered plea did no good.

"You have to!" This last came in a shriek as his chest rose and fell one last time and was still. His skin grew cold beneath her hands.

"No, Luke. Luke." She clutched him, leaning as close as possible. "Don't leave! Please, Luke. Don't go. It's my fault," she babbled, tears streaming down her face. "I know 'tis. I should hae taken better care o' you. I love you. I'll do better. I promise I'll do better, if you'll only just wake up. Smile at me one more time, little brother. Luke? Luke!"

But it was too late. She knew it by his unnatural stillness, the cold clamminess of his skin, the blue that was deeper than ever before in his lips and fingernails.

"Rosalind." She felt Ewan's warm hand on her shoulder, heard his deep, melancholy tones. " 'Tis over. He's gone."

"No!" The heartbroken whisper was all she managed before the swirling darkness claimed her thoughts.

❧

At the parson's house, Ewan covered Rosalind with his own coat and sat by the fire to wait. She'd revived fairly quickly, though not before his own heart had skipped a beat in mortal dread. They'd made it through the short burial before she cried herself into unconsciousness once again. The train had moved on and wouldn't be taking them home to Saddleback. Arthur and Kaitlin wouldn't have even the cold comfort of burying their son.

"I brought you some tea to warm your bones." The parson's wife whisked in and set down the tray. "Though I'm afraid it won't help with the sorrow. Only God's grace and His time will lessen that burden." She glanced around before leaving them alone in the small parlor.

With Rosalind sleeping, Ewan had no company but his own grief, which came rushing forward in the silence. Tears welled in his eyes as he thought of lively little Luke, so welcoming, such a blessing to his family. He remembered how the boy had welcomed him to the table, threw snowballs with reckless abandon, skated as though he hoped to fly off the ice, and bolted down frozen maple syrup with more enthusiasm than sense.

Gone. Lost to us forever. Why, God? He buried his head in his hands, trying to swallow the tears and the pain. *Why now? Why Luke? I understand Your wanting him by Your side, but could You not hae spared him to us for a while longer, knowing he was Yours for all time?* He struggled to understand, to accept, but failed. It seemed like years he sat in the chair, trying to fathom the reasons why Luke should be robbed of his life and his family stripped of their joy. No understanding came.

"Luke." Rosalind stirred, her eyes opening. For an all-too-brief moment, she seemed fine. Then remembrance clouded the bright blue, and she hugged her knees to her chest. "He's gone."

"Yes." Ewan walked over to sit beside her, drawing her close to offer what little solace he could. "He's gone to be with our heavenly Father now. We'll see him again someday."

"I know," she whispered. "But it doesn't make it easier today." She drew a shaky breath. "At least—at least he's where each breath he draws doesn't pain him. He's beyond the reach of that now. 'Tis all I can think of to be glad about."

" 'Tis no small thing," he soothed. "We always want what's best for the ones we love. Luke has that, and we should rejoice that he's found peace and joy with our Savior."

"Yes." She straightened her shoulders a little. "He's happy. I should be happy for him. And I am." She looked up at him, her eyes shining with tears once more. " 'Tis myself, and Mam and Da and Grandmam, that I grieve for. 'Tis our loss."

"Aye." Ewan rubbed his hand over her back. " 'Tis certainly

our loss. But, Rosalind"—he tipped her chin to keep her gaze fixed on him—"'tisn't your fault."

"Ewan"—she tried to pull away from him—"you don't understand. . . ."

"I understand better than you think." He moved to cup her cheek with his palm. "You watched o'er him as best you could, and he cherished your love. There was nothing you could do about his weak lungs, or the illness, save stay by his side and offer what comfort and aid you could. You did all of that."

"No." She shook her head so vehemently that she freed herself from his grasp. "I could hae done more. I should hae watched him more closely. I shouldna hae fallen asleep. I should hae—" She gasped back a sob. "I should hae shown him every moment how much he meant to me—how I loved him."

"You did, Rosalind." He took her fidgeting hands in his. "It may not feel that way now, but you did. Wi' every smile, every snowball, every mug of hot cider. . .you loved him each day he was wi' us. I saw it, and I know he did, too."

"Do you think so?" She met his gaze, seeking reassurance.

"I'm certain." He shifted a tiny bit. "His life was never ours to keep, Rosalind." His eyes stung. "No one's is."

"Ewan?" Her gaze was searching. "What—what made you say that last part? Are you feeling poorly?" Her voice rose as she pressed the back of her hand to his forehead. "We'll call Dr. Carmichael again. . . ."

"No." He captured her hand and held it. "I wasn't referring to myself. I thought of my mother." He saw that she waited for him to share more. *Maybe my experience will help her through the grief,* he reasoned. *Besides, there's nothing I want hidden betwixt us.*

"When I was about Luke's age"—he winced at her hiss of

indrawn breath but continued—"my da left Ireland to seek his fortune in America. He charged me to look after Mam and look after things while he was away. He planned to send money back to us so we could book passage to join him."

"Go on."

"It seems that Da was one of many, many men who had the same idea. Work was harder to find than he'd anticipated, and it took longer to gather the money. Months passed, then years. I worked at odd jobs—smithing, shoeing, whatever I could be paid to turn a hand to—and managed to keep food on the table and a roof o'er our heads. Every scrap o' money Da sent, we saved to buy our fare. But every day, the light in Mam's eyes dimmed just a wee bit more. She missed Da so."

"It must hae been hard for you both." She squeezed his hand.

"Aye, 'twas." He took a deep breath. "Finally, I could no longer bear watching her fade away before my eyes from missing him. As the man of the house, I made the decision to use our money for a single ticket. I sent her ahead, alone. The plan was for me to follow later. She gave me her wedding band, the only thing she owned of any value. If I needed to, she instructed me to sell it."

"How wonderful of you." She nestled close. "So selfless of you—to send your mam back to your da and ask to be left all alone. Such love. Your parents must hae been proud."

"No." The words thickened in his throat, but he managed to grind them out. "Mam never stepped foot on the American shore. Alone on a miserable ship, she caught an illness on board. Wi' no one to look after her, she died during the voyage."

"Oh, Ewan." Her grip tightened. "That wasn't your fault." She spoke with fierce conviction. "You have to know that."

"I didn't know"—his voice became hoarse—"I didn't know about her death until Da wrote me. The letter reprimanded me for sending Mam alone when he'd left her in my care. 'Twas the last I ever heard from him." He ignored her shocked gasp and plowed ahead. "I saved money on my own, refusing to sell Mam's ring. When I made it to America, I spent years searching for him, but it didn't work." He paused and choked out the final words. "I don't even know whether or not he's still alive."

"Ewan." She held his head to her shoulder and rocked back and forth. "You can't blame yourself for your mother's death. You did the best you could by her. 'Twasn't fair o' your father to lash out at you. I'm sure 'twas done only in grief."

"Perhaps." He straightened up. "I've never told anyone about this." He traced the band of gold adorning her finger. "But you wear her ring, and you are to bear my name. We should hae no secrets betwixt us. And just as I had to come to terms wi' my mam's death, so, too, do you hae to stop blaming yourself for Luke's."

"Luke. . ." Her face fell at the mention of her brother.

"You did the best you could by him," Ewan softly echoed her own words. " 'Tisn't fair to blame yourself in your grief."

Silence stretched between them for a long while.

Finally, Rosalind spoke. "You're right." They sat for a while longer. "Ewan?"

"Yes, Rosalind?"

"Not too long ago, I was reading Da's Bible. I looked at the death records—and the marriage lines—and wondered what our future held."

"Oh?"

"And I turned to one o' my favorite chapters—Ecclesiastes 3."

" 'To every thing there is a season,'" he recited along with her, " 'and a time to every purpose under the heaven: A time to be born, and a time to die.'" They both stopped.

"And I thought how strange it was, that in the family records, birth and death are placed side by side and that it is the same in the scriptures." She bit her lip. "Ewan? When we have a son—"

"We'll name him Luke," he finished firmly. She nodded, a ghost of a smile breaking through her grief. "Rosalind, that chapter continues until it comes to another portion I think applies here."

" 'A time to laugh; a time to mourn'?" she asked. "For now is certainly the time to mourn."

"Aye, 'tis." He threaded his fingers through her hair. "Though I was thinking of the part that says, 'a time to lose; a time to keep.'"

"Oh." Rosalind thought for a moment. "We've lost Luke. What is there to keep? Our grief?" She seemed despondent at the very thought.

"No, though Luke will always be in our hearts." Ewan waited until her gaze met his. "You and I, Rosalind. Our love. The beginning of our life together. That is what we are to keep—hope for the future and trust that the Lord will see us through."

"Oh, Ewan." She kissed his cheek. "How right you are. And that is the way Luke would hae wanted it—that we allow for grief but look forward to the promise of tomorrow."

"And when we wed, my Rosalind," Ewan vowed, " 'twill be a time to keep."

epilogue

Montana, 1889

"Can you believe it?" Marlene squealed, all but dancing for joy. "After two years of waiting, I'm finally married!"

"Wi' a home already built and a farm already in operation. Johnny's worked hard to make ready for his beautiful bride." Rosalind smiled. "I'm thinking 'twon't be long before you join your mam and me." She patted her rounded tummy with affection and looked at Delana, who was two months farther along. "Isn't that right, Mrs. Freimont?"

"Ja." Delana laughed. "Though I hadn't thought to bear a babe near the time when my daughter would!"

"It's a wonderful surprise." Marlene leaned over her mother's swollen stomach. "She's going to be a sister, I think."

"Not mine." Rosalind cupped her hands over her own swollen midriff. "I bear a son. Ewan and I—we've decided to name him Luke." Her eyes sparkled more with joy than sorrow, a sign of God's healing and the passage of time.

"What a wonderful idea!" Mam drew her into a tight clasp, her own eyes looking suspiciously moist. "Luke would hae liked that."

"Yes, he would." Marlene reached out to grasp both of their hands. "It's a lovely gesture, and I'm so happy for you!"

"We'll speak of it more when the babes are born." Delana smiled. "For now, we've much to celebrate. My daughter, a bride, and Montana declared an official state!"

"Yes. It's a grand day for a wedding—a day to be remembered." Johnny came up behind the women to steal a kiss from his blushing bride. "We're going to blow the anvils now."

They all hurried to the clearing, where Ewan and Johnny carefully overturned one anvil, pouring black gunpowder into the base's hollow before positioning the second anvil directly atop it. A thin trail of the gunpowder spilled over the side, waiting to be lit.

"And here we go! Everybody step far back, out of the way!" Johnny lit the trail of powder and rushed to Marlene's side. At that moment, the anvils began to dance, emitting a loud series of sparks until the pressure built up sufficiently to overturn the top anvil with a spectacular *boom!*

When the gunpowder supply was exhausted—and everyone's ears rang with the sound of the merry tradition—Ewan stepped forward. Rosalind watched with pride as her husband waited for everyone's attention and began his speech.

"When I married my beautiful Rosalind o'er a year ago, 'twas a day of great joy. And also one tempered wi' sorrow wi' young Luke"—he paused for a moment as several people drew shaky breaths—"gone to heaven. But we know he would hae wanted us to celebrate."

He broke into a grin. "Now, after a long, patient wait, Johnny and Marlene hae wed on this joyous day. I'm both pleased and honored to speak an old Irish blessing upon their marriage and on all who are gathered here today. If my wife would join me. . ." He held out his hand, beckoning Rosalind to come to his side.

Surprised, she did so. Suddenly, she knew he'd planned the blessing to be a celebration of their own marriage, as much as Johnny and Marlene's. Looking into the deep green of his gaze, she spoke the ancient words with him:

> *"May love and laughter light your days,*
> *and warm your heart and home.*
> *May good and faithful friends be yours,*
> *wherever you may roam.*
> *May peace and plenty bless your world*
> *with joy that long endures.*
> *May all life's passing seasons bring*
> *the best to you and yours."*

A Letter To Our Readers

Dear Reader:

In order that we might better contribute to your reading enjoyment, we would appreciate your taking a few minutes to respond to the following questions. We welcome your comments and read each form and letter we receive. When completed, please return to the following:

Fiction Editor
Heartsong Presents
PO Box 719
Uhrichsville, Ohio 44683

1. Did you enjoy reading *A Time to Keep* by Kelly Eileen Hake?
   ❑ Very much! I would like to see more books by this author!
   ❑ Moderately. I would have enjoyed it more if

   _____

   _____

   _____

2. Are you a member of **Heartsong Presents**? ❑ Yes ❑ No
   If no, where did you purchase this book? _____

   _____

3. How would you rate, on a scale from 1 (poor) to 5 (superior), the cover design? _____

4. On a scale from 1 (poor) to 10 (superior), please rate the following elements.

   _____ Heroine   _____ Plot
   _____ Hero   _____ Inspirational theme
   _____ Setting   _____ Secondary characters

5. These characters were special because? _____

_____

_____

6. How has this book inspired your life? _____

_____

_____

7. What settings would you like to see covered in future
   Heartsong Presents books? _____

_____

_____

8. What are some inspirational themes you would like to see
   treated in future books? _____

_____

_____

9. Would you be interested in reading other **Heartsong
   Presents** titles? ❏ Yes ❏ No

10. Please check your age range:
     ❏ Under 18   ❏ 18-24
     ❏ 25-34   ❏ 35-45
     ❏ 46-55   ❏ Over 55

Name _____

Occupation _____

Address _____

City, State, Zip_____

CALIFORNIA BRIDES

3 stories in 1

Three Chance women find love in California.

Stories by author Cathy Marie Hake include: *Hardful of Flowers*, *Bridal Veil*, and *No Buttons or Beaux*.

Historical, paperback, 352 pages, 5³⁄₁₆" x 8"

_____

Please send me _____ copies of *California Brides*. I am enclosing $6.97 for each. (Please add $3.00 to cover postage and handling per order. OH add 7% tax. If outside the U.S. please call 740-922-7280 for shipping charges.)

Name_____

Address _____

City, State, Zip _____

Presents

___HP663	Journeys, T. H. Murray		___HP716	Spinning Out of Control, V. McDonough
___HP664	Chance Adventure, K. E. Hake			
___HP667	Sagebrush Christmas, B. L. Etchison		___HP719	Weaving a Future, S. P. Davis
___HP668	Duel Love, B. Youree		___HP720	Bridge Across the Sea, P. Griffin
___HP671	Sooner or Later, V. McDonough		___HP723	Adam's Bride, L. Harris
___HP672	Chance of a Lifetime, K. E. Hake		___HP724	A Daughter's Quest, L. N. Dooley
___HP675	Bayou Secrets, K. M. Y'Barbo		___HP727	Wyoming Hoofbeats, S. P. Davis
___HP676	Beside Still Waters, T. V. Bateman		___HP728	A Place of Her Own, L. A. Coleman
___HP679	Rose Kelly, J. Spaeth		___HP731	The Bounty Hunter and the Bride, V. McDonough
___HP680	Rebecca's Heart, L. Harris			
___HP683	A Gentlemen's Kiss, K. Comeaux		___HP732	Lonely in Longtree, J. Stengl
___HP684	Copper Sunrise, C. Cox		___HP735	Deborah, M. Colvin
___HP687	The Ruse, T. H. Murray		___HP736	A Time to Plant, K. E. Hake
___HP688	A Handful of Flowers, C. M. Hake		___HP740	The Castaway's Bride, S. P. Davis
___HP691	Bayou Dreams, K. M. Y'Barbo		___HP741	Golden Dawn, C. M. Hake
___HP692	The Oregon Escort, S. P. Davis		___HP743	Broken Bow, I. Brand
___HP695	Into the Deep, L. Bliss		___HP744	Golden Days, M. Connealy
___HP696	Bridal Veil, C. M. Hake		___HP747	A Wealth Beyond Riches, V. McDonough
___HP699	Bittersweet Remembrance, G. Fields			
___HP700	Where the River Flows, I. Brand		___HP748	Golden Twilight, K. Y'Barbo
___HP703	Moving the Mountain, Y. Lehman		___HP751	The Music of Home, T. H. Murray
___HP704	No Buttons or Beaux, C. M. Hake		___HP752	Tara's Gold, L. Harris
___HP707	Mariah's Hope, M. J. Conner		___HP755	Journey to Love, L. Bliss
___HP708	The Prisoner's Wife, S. P. Davis		___HP756	The Lumberjack's Lady, S. P. Davis
___HP711	A Gentle Fragrance, F. Griffin		___HP759	Stirring Up Romance, J. L. Barton
___HP712	Spoke of Love, C. M. Hake		___HP760	Mountains Stand Strong, I. Brand
___HP715	Vera's Turn for Love, T. H. Murray			

Great Inspirational Romance at a Great Price!

Heartsong Presents books are inspirational romances in contemporary and historical settings, designed to give you an enjoyable, spirit-lifting reading experience. You can choose wonderfully written titles from some of today's best authors like Peggy Darty, Sally Laity, DiAnn Mills, Colleen L. Reece, Debra White Smith, and many others.

When ordering quantities less than twelve, above titles are $2.97 each.
Not all titles may be available at time of order.

SEND TO: **Heartsong Presents** Reader's Service
                P.O. Box 721, Uhrichsville, Ohio 44683

Please send me the items checked above. I am enclosing $ _____
(please add $3.00 to cover postage per order. OH add 7% tax. NJ
add 6%). Send check or money order, no cash or C.O.D.s, please.
       To place a credit card order, call 1-740-922-7280.

NAME _____

ADDRESS _____

CITY/STATE _____ ZIP _____